To build a bridge between generations and
promote communication with world.

Foreword

We identify ourselves as the first-generation immigrants who refuse to give up writing poems, essays, and novels in the Korean language in the past quarter-century, despite the hardship of making a living here in the United States.

All of us made our literary debuts in Korea by winning new writer's awards from Korean journals and newspapers, and a few published their works in English in the past.

When I talked to my colleagues and friends about my plan to publish the first English edition of Korean literature, they responded with, "No kidding. I have never heard of anyone doing something like that."

I understand that it is not easy to publish a collection of Korean literary works in English, because the majority of our members speak exclusively Korean, not English.

My intention in publishing this English edition of Korean literature is to introduce our hearts and souls to the next generation and society as a whole so that we can communicate easier and promote understanding with one another. This is the first step to conveying our group consciousness to multiple ethnic groups.

In 2014, Korean American Writers Association of Eastern USA won the Byeng-Ju Lee International Literary Award 2014 which boosted our pride and courage and motivated us to publish Korean literature in English.

I would like to thank Dr. Hong Ai Bai at Long Island University for her sincere effort in editing, as well as Jung Sook Yang and Ryo Noh, essayists, for their devotion for the first English edition of *New York Literature*.

Woon Ha (Edward Ha, M.D.)
President
Korean American Writers Association of Eastern USA

Contents

Poems

Jung Sook Byun: After the Flowers Fade / Subway Environ 1	3
Sung Ja Cho: Punching Bag / Painkiller	6
Im Sun Choi: Prayer	8
Chie Ja Chun: Umbilical Cord	9
Woon Ha: New York 911 / The Reeds Immortal	10
Mi Kwang Hwang: Gaps	12
Annie Aeja Jun: Autumn and Jazz / The Hike	13
Tae Soo Kim: Paper Coffee Cup / Salmon Caught by Fishing Pole	15
Sang Hee Kwak: Another Winter Tale / The Desire to Sit Lower	19
Chung Kang Lee: The Kite 2 / Trees, Brimming with Expectations	21
Hye Ran Lee: Landscape of Last Day of the Year / Chosen (Korean) Zucchini	25
Sung Kon Lee: Snow Day	29
Ji Hye Shin: Water	30
Kwan Ho Yun: City Seagulls / Thanksgiving Day	32
Young Mi Yun: Blue Pine Tree / Ice Flower	34
C H Park (Pian Zhenhua): The Unfinished Love / Often	36
Ja Won Kim: Buddha's Birthday	38

Essays

Gloria Cha: My Little Doctor / The Key to Heaven	43
Eun Sil Chung: Beauty of One Sip of Coffee	48
Ki Hoon Kim: The Belly Button / Pennies with Purpose	51
Min Jung Kim: A Happy Life / Leftover Space	59
Myong Soon Kim: The Birdhouse / Valentine's Day	65
Oak Soo Kim: Finding Miss Beefus	73
Chune Hee Lee: Shakespeare in the Park / The Liberation of Growing Old	82
Hea Sook Lim: Whispering Walls / Letters Sent in Winter	86
Jung Kil Na: Our Lifelong Search for Fun	91
Ryo Noh : Locking Eyes with Columbus	93
Jung Sook Yang: Open House / New Family	96
Bong Won Yeon: Carnival in Brazil	103

Stories

Soo Sup Byun: Wanted God	109
Min Jung Kim: Practicing to Depart	146

POEMS

After the Flowers Fade
Jung Sook Byun

The flowers wilt.
The shadows of the white flowers fade.
The flowers wilt, and
The joy that once blossomed radiantly
Flutters downward,
Taking with it the vibrant memories of the white butterfly petals.
As the rippling shadows of the white flowers vanish
Upon desolation after desolation,
The tree
Tries its best to grow leaves round and green.
Gradually
Those that clung on to the wounds of separation
Sprout from painful scars as they vanish.
A budding apple
Bites at the nipple of the vanishing flowers
And ripens sweetly,
Intoxicated by its fragrance.
The flowers that conceived another joy before fading
Are no longer in memory.

Subway Environs 1
Jung Sook Byun

At the Grand Central Terminal,
Commuting crowds flow and ebb like water,
A running river
From where they come to where they go.
No one says a word.

Whether a sign condemns them to silence as they head toward the exits,
Whether with cheerful, dark, heavy, or light footsteps
All at different paces,
All flowing toward their day-to-day routine—
Silently. Silently.

Following the path of silence,
A man creates sound.
Without flowing like the rest, a solitary figure
Plays the violin,
Breaking the rule of silence
With a high and clear lilt.
The man plays the strings,
Or maybe the strings play the man.
The melody rises like smoke and settles
In beautiful blue,
Embracing tired shoulders
And nipping the heels of busy people,
Inviting dialogue.

The violin case,
Filled with a few indifferent coins and bills—
Perhaps
The conversations will begin.

jungsook.byun@gmail.com

Punching Bag
Sung Ja Cho (Jane Yoo)

On the curbside with some household trash
Stands a punching bag, looking up at the autumn sun
As if receiving a standing ovation.

Taking punches is its destiny.
Strong and stout, perhaps it endured some
Teenager's angst,
Perhaps made a champion out of a promising boxer,
Put a crown of life on someone.
Now facing death, as it sometimes comes too early to genius minds.
Underneath the scars, it holds history
Worth many volumes,
Says a woman while punching it firmly.

Then it screams,
"Yes, I lived. With no regrets."

Painkiller
Sung Ja Cho (Jane Yoo)

My eyes open
into lights too bright.
"Mommy!" I hear.
"You're awake!" Next,
cells asleep
now stand up
straight like sorghum straws—
my babies.
My son's arm I grab
pulses under muscles
of a boy, almost—
such a baby, too young to know.
What a concern on the faces of big sisters.
Which faraway planet did you come back from,
to walk along with me in this life,
to carry me through this moment of sadness?
I say no to inflowing morphine.
They are my painkiller.
Strong enough.
Reason enough.

jbbyoo@hotmail.com

Prayer
Im Sun Choi

While hardening my way to go
with a sorrow of the wind,
sweat of a lump of burning charcoal inside a blazing inferno,
I pray on my knees.

Please keep my poverty hidden under the skin,
hardly to be found.

I have holes all over my heart
from the iron-sand wind of desert; the flesh gets crumbled,
as reason, an inch short of forgiveness,
does not allow me to become a loveless stone pillar.

Do not allow my desire, the sleeping yearning,
to be awakened again
by a creaking sound of the kneecap.

My beloved angels,
embrace the stone, gravely field on the way of immigration;
do not allow me to walk a bumpy road,
and guide me to the sea of overflowing grace …

Umbilical Cord
Chie Ja Chun

In the heart of peace,
There was Grand Northern Policy.
The South and the North
Are a vein tied by an umbilical cord.
Undulating waves rise on the Dae Dong River.

On the fallen leaves in a far foreign land,
The child in thirst
Wets his throat,
Gazes at the continent through the fetal movements.
The light of possibility reinforces the life
And truly longs for life with deep breathing.

Sunshine of an encounter,
That policy
Placed the bridge of understanding.
The thirst of oxygen
Ignites the flame by the umbilical cord,
Strokes the graft line,
Sowing maternal seeds on the umbilical cord.
The waiting for unification
Recreates the roots.

chiechun1004@gmail.com

New York 911
Woon Ha

Willy, Tom!
What is happening? How is it speakable?
Holding the sky up with your arms at the corner
of our village, welcoming anyone and everyone
who comes across the oceans and over the mountains,
you were hit by burning arrows.
We are choked, choked up.
Crying at the top of your voice, "Here's freedom!
Your dream is here."
Why do black moths fly on a beautiful morning?
Willy, Tom!
So many posters on the wall with the heart-aching stories,
searching, for you are getting wet in the fall rain.
Is it bleeding or tearing deep inside me?
Emptiness without you is hanging in the sky,
piercing through my heart,
as if the burning arrows strike again.
Holding my tears back, I find myself so much
in love with you and this town,
no longer an outsider.
No one would dare to take our freedom and dream away
again.

The Reeds Immortal
Woon Ha

Reeds on the bank of the River Nile
are tirelessly standing since ancient time,
Listening in the wind to those
who took a journey to Eternity.
They are still on their journey, not in vain.
Reeds wave the sun to rise from the Red Sea,
push it to cross the river.
There are numerous pyramids
rising and falling in the stream.
Smile at the sun sunk into the Sahara Desert.
What if the sun does not cross?
No one shall expect eternity;
One disappears forever as ash instead.
Ambition of mankind once flowed on the River Nile;
shall it be not coming back
to those who have overloaded ambition?
At sundown,
reeds begin their dream endless for the morrow
and the morrow.

poethawoon@gmail.com

Gaps
Mi Kwang Hwang

Water flows through
the gaps in the world

My thoughts flow through
the gaps in my body

Our love grows through
the gaps between us

There is forgiveness
because there are gaps
between words and actions

Another day also finds us
between the gaps

hamikwang@gmail.com

Autumn and Jazz
Annie Jun

One, two, three …
Autumn is taking shots of soju.

The leaves turn red from the
Caress of the tipsy season.

The drunken trees begin to shake,
Causing a shower of leaves.

The piling, scattering
And piling movements of leaves look
Like they are doing a makchum,

Drunken from the Fall Festival.
The sound of a trumpet
Awkwardly played by a poet can be heard.

Oh! It turns out to be jazz music,
Calling for fall.

I join the fall and dance to the jazz music.

Winter, on the other hand, is waiting afar
With excitement for its turn.

The Hike
Annie Jun

The sound of stepping on the fallen leaves
Shakes the mountain;
The smell in the air is fragrant.

The burning fall blurs the boundaries
Of the forest and mountain and
Dyes the hikers red.

The reeds that fill the lake
Watch the day deteriorate
And cling onto each other
In hopes of staying together.

The water as clear as the skin
Seen through a sheer shirt
Is flowing through the pebbles.

I stand on top of the mountain;
The narrow path ahead is foreign.
Suddenly a familiar feeling embraces me.

annieree123@hotmail.com

Paper Coffee Cup
Tae Soo Kim

Enormous rains and snowstorms invaded our global villages; Japan was swept by a formidable tsunami.

In front of the terminal TV, people focus on the news coverage showing the devastation caused by "water-bombs" while holding their breaths and drinking coffee out of their paper cups.

At a logging site in the Amazon.

After the day when our friends fell to the ground, shrieking with their lower trunks mercilessly cut, they were sold to a foreign land; soon they became heartwarming paper cups that disappear like breaths in the air without a trace.

Just like me, they were sold and destroyed, melted and burned, only to leave behind a bitter-sour odor.

Only beholding once the sacredness of my existence, I leave behind the trace of my being stained with blood and burned or buried.

That place called the Amazon, which has sustained its existence from the beginning of the earth, and where I have been standing all this time, is being engulfed in flames in the name of "development."

Being raped and deformed even to the roots. I encountered immeasurable pains; teardrops bombard the top of the falling and sliding dirt.

Even today, people still drink the vending-machine coffee with paper cups, worrying about things like global warming, heavy rain, radioactive contamination, causing inflation in agricultural and seafood products.

Salmon Caught by Fishing Pole
Tae Soo Kim

Frozen dregs buried deep in me, trying to melt with the sunshine, I stand by the riverbank.

A group of salmon is coming home with blossoming water flowers behind them, trying to rest themselves under the roots of reincarnation.

Struggling to survive, they quietly conquer the angry currents; their stomachs intertwine with the whiteness of the river water and their backs became blue, bruised by the ocean's tides.

Shattered but recommitting, following the almost-forgotten tiny calling.

Holding on to the never-drying flow, they carefully maneuver their fins; they withstand this unfamiliar world.

Maybe, realizing their destiny of no return, and in the midst of mundane daily lives, and for the sake of "coming" lives, they, without hesitance, bite the lure of a fishing pole.

In order to become the offering of the fisherman, they nonchalantly throw themselves in the air after racing to live through death …

When the happy facial complexion is tickled by the wind, times gone by float atop like a mirage.

The cobalt sky penetrates their eyes.

A new sky is opening up.

tae_soo_kim@hotmail.com

Another Winter Tale
Sang Hee Kwak

Were
death,
injury,
despair,
hope,
hate,
love,
and love's linking
confined in time's jar
that no longer shatters?
Were they cut into particles,
smaller than dust motes,
smaller than the heart of darkness,
and confined as unseen light and shadow?
In the center of fire, there is a drop of water;
all the fire's force is windowed,
flies around the sky.
The smallest bit of shadow
beginning again from zero,
now at last the tender grass extends its leaves.

The Desire to Sit Lower
Sang Hee Kwak

To the crumbled sands under the feet of men and beasts, sweet-smelling wind
to quivering petals, grass of sidewalks,
to the moon at the end of the month,
to the books, poetry, my first and last poems,
to my breath, my feet, my hands,
to you who do not see me leave you,
to laughter,
to tears,
to handshaking—
Alas, to shining water drops of early morning,
to you standing at corner of the other side of road,
to yesterday's torn newspapers,
to the sounds of a kettle boiling water in the deep winter,
to the warm hand upon my shoulder,
to someone drooping his head, lost in the midtown of Broadway,
to despair, despair never filled,
to a little child's twinkling eyes,
to the winter flower garden,
to the winter grove,
to the color fading away,
to the sound without sound,
to the darkness, to the light,
to the uphill of debts never ending …

kwaksanghee9@gmail.com

The Kite II
Chung Kang Lee (Kim)

The kite, encircled with a Taegeuk* band around its forehead,
of wide-open soaring spirit,

Dances freely,
crashing against the wind.

Retraces the steps of loss,
riding the air of remorse.

From each torn-off or cut-out spot
comes sorrow that brings birth of new flesh.
Why didn't I realize it was the blessing?
How futile hiding and veiling is!

The wind,
Embracing freedom,
Billows the spirit of the deceased.

The unforgettable world affairs seen from a distance,
the pierced moments in my mind—
I turned them into your song,
In the manner of flapping wings.

Its forehead is
the bursting brilliance
and the communication of an eternal tail.

*Taeguek is the Great Absolute (the source of the dual principal of yin and yang).

Trees, Brimming with Expectation
Chung Kang Lee (Kim)

Trees
chatting, singing,
rubbing head-to-head all day long,
even after prayers, weeping,
standing upright again at the same spot
with a clear face once the dark clouds roll away.

The canopy invites the heavens
once weaving the interlace of sunlight
along with the beckoning of the gentle wind,
raking the waves in the sea far away
with the bird's nest,
gliding to the cozy haven of night rest …

Even a piece of falling soul
is hidden behind the folding screen of noon
after watching the beginning and end of
the transparent meeting.

When the stars
toast one another at the festival
with the barefoot dance of the possessed …

Forgotten moments
Are now revived and hands shaken
each night as the moon rises;
relish the passionate embrace.

Spiritual songs spurt up
from the sap
collected from the essence of life ...

mkim99@nyc.rr.com

Landscape of the Last Day of the Year
Hyeran Lee Yu

It's not just the year
That comes and goes
Like the blinding radiance of the sun in the night sky.
Manhattan Times Square's crystal ball,
In the last seconds of counting down, that very moment
In the St. John Medical Center in Ohio
New lives are birthed.
Weary bodies lie back down,
Some to take their last breaths,
All over the world.
As fireworks burst in splendor,
The hospital rooms burst full
Though none were invited.
Those wistfully zealous for life
Approach the end of this world
In various languages,
Lift the same prayer,
And withered hearts beat frail,
Stained with the color of heaven
In the solitude of life's coming and going.
Sacred petitions
Gleam brighter than fireworks,
Becoming prayers
As they reach higher and higher
Into the night sky.
It's not just the year
That comes and goes.

Inspiration for the Poem
On the last day of 2014, I worked at St. John Medical Center in Ohio as a chaplain intern. Although the whole world was in a festive mood for the New Year, the hospital was quiet. The patients could not return to their homes or enjoy time with their families. I realized although America is a multicultural, multiethnic, and multireligious country, all the patients in the hospital prayed the same prayer.

Choseon (Korean) Zucchini
Hyeran Lee Yu

A plot in the backyard
Bears a piece of homeland of hers.
Visiting a far-off village in dreams,
Aching for home,
She turns up the dirt
On this foreign soil
Where she knows her body will rest someday
And buries seeds deep inside this desolate earth,
Reclaiming another homeland.
Yellow blossoms on every vine,
A glimpse of the familiar patch—
Friendly faces, cherished images,
Dreams that refuse to fade out in time.
As each bud grows in full,
Their weathered hands with swollen knuckles
Hand me a piece of homeland.
A wicker basket overflowing
With Choseon zucchini
Paired with her innocent smile—
My heart starts weeping.

Inspiration for the Poem
When I moved to America, I was surprised to see that some Korean women had planted vegetable gardens in their backyards, despite the demanding stresses of their jobs, their children, and their household duties. I met

such diligent, generous women as they showered me with Korean zucchini, sesame leaves, hot peppers, and leaf lettuce, all homegrown and fresh from their gardens. These women had been living in America for the past twenty or thirty years, and yet they still resembled the typical Korean woman. They cultivated this foreign soil, transforming it into a homeland away from home. They learned to transform what was an unsettling immigrant life into a life of abundance. Truly, they are beautiful women.

hyeranleeyu@yahoo.com

Snowy Day
Sung Kon Lee

A scene covered by white snow is how the camera sees the world,
A totally black-and-white photo.

That night in my dream,
I saw a black-and-white photo with nostalgic childhood faces.
They were waiving to me with a bright smile, asking me to join them.

I am so eager to move back in time.
The sunlight awakes me.
Before the snow melts and the world goes back to its own color,
My exhausted body longs for deep sleep,
To return to that faded black-and-white photo.

sklee4262@yahoo.com

Water
Ji Hye Shin

I am water.
A nomad, a droplet
adrift on an aimless wind
having roamed about the universe
lays its weary body on a river
without rent flesh, without shattered bones,
rejoins the others in an unified embrace
and goes to the ocean
floating on the swell of the sea,
sleeping like the dead.
Abandons the world
along with a salt-embedded wind,
endless sky,
a canopy of heaven above
coming through its rattling doors.
A drop ripe with the smell of life
swims through stars and space,
a journey through deep night, parted clouds
turning into another drop of water
once again turning into a river,
then an ocean.
Solid seeds of water,

even if evaporated, cannot be destroyed,
neither in the midst of the unadorned atmosphere
nor in the core of earth that penetrates the planet
in this world and the next,
an interminable life.
I am only water.

shinjihyepoet@hanmail.net

City Seagulls
Kwan Ho Yun

Around our neighborhood McDonald's
Seagulls flock from time to time.

Seagulls should live in the sea.
Seagulls should not live around restaurants.

Do not try to live comfortably;
Go back to the rocking blue sea.

Despite the storm and deep waters,
Elegantly snatch the fresh fishes

With courage and challenge.
Beyond the trials and tribulations,
Sing delightfully.

Thanksgiving Day
Kwan Ho Yun

While walking around the neighborhood,
I thank the sky.
I thank the earth.
I thank all who live in this day and age.
I especially thank each person
For sharing emotions together.

garyyun1001@gmail.com

Blue Pine Tree
Young Mi Yun

For a million years,

even if the wind blows,

shall become the sky one looks up to

Even if
today
and tomorrow
never meet hand in hand—

Shall scatter
unashamed
fragrance of mine

In each heart of light,
shall deeply engrave
this blueness.

Overlooking the blue sky
for eons
shall be
deeply rooted blueness.

Ice Flower
Young Mi Yun

Alaska's ancient ice—
within the iceberg, a bloomed flower

fragile from
small movement.
The body shall break into a pink hue
to become a blossom,

a tale to be told in hiding.

Who would break my dreams?
Who could abolish my legend?

Ground-breaking sound,
the flowing sound of melted ice mountain—
my love,
are you listening to that sound?

poet.yunyoungmi@gmail.com

Unfinished Love
C. H. Park (Piao, Zhenhua)

The small leaf knows the wind,
Shakes trembling heart.

The flower in the field knows the dew,
Swallows an early morning's sadness.

The dragonfly flies calmly
As my heart looks for you.

I weep
For our unfinished love.

Often
C. H. Park (Piao, Zhenhua)

I often wanted to be in your heart,
Like a crying seven-year-old kid.

I often wanted to lie down
Beside a still pool with your lullaby.

I often wanted your arm as my pillow,
Lying on the beach, fondled by the wind.

I often wanted to build a sandcastle
As the seal of our love.

chparkkr@gmail.com

Buddha's Birthday
Ja Won Kim

Dear …

As it is,
You reached perfection
Through silence,
Like a Sumi Mountain.

Your guidance
Shines radiantly;
Millions cry
For their happiness.

Clarity of mind is
The only freedom.
Tears fall from eyes
And sorrow falls from the body;

He made me the way I am
And taught me how to walk.
We're all
Rooted together,

As is nature,
As is the living world.
Those who seek the Dharma
Take solace in knowing

He will always hold your hand.
You're always with us;
Thank you, Buddha.
Happy Buddha's birthday.

jawonyoga@hotmail.com

ESSAYS

My Little Doctor
Gloria Cha

My little doctor gave me two injections in my buttocks today. My doctor is my three-year-old granddaughter.

Whenever I catch a cold, I tell my doctor "I have a fever" or "I have a headache" or "I have a sore throat." Sometimes I might have a stuffy nose or a runny nose.

This is how a routine checkup goes. First, my little doctor looks at me with her big plastic glasses on. She puts on her plastic toy stethoscope to check my chest and back. Instructing me, "Open your mouth," she looks into my mouth and ears with a flashlight. Then she writes on a small piece of paper. When I ask her what it is, my doctor says, "It's for medicine." She writes a prescription for me. She tells me to pull up my clothes so that she can give me an injection with her plastic syringe.

If I pretend that the injection is causing pain by saying "Ow-wee! Ow-wee!" she puts a bandage on where it hurts.

Then my three-year-old doctor tells me, "Good girl! Good job!" After that, she gives me a Mickey Mouse sticker on my left arm.

Today, after receiving two plastic injections in my buttocks, my cold seems to be getting better. I don't know how many more injections my little doctor will give me. It doesn't matter, however, because receiving treatment from my little doctor is so much fun! The best thing about my doctor is her pristinely clear spirit, which clears my spirit too. I love my little doctor very much.

The Key to Heaven
Gloria Cha

Nowadays, everyone carries a key, from kindergarteners to adults. When I was a young girl growing up in Korea, there was no such thing as a key to the house. The house door was locked from the inside by a horizontal stick, and when a visitor wanted to come in, a knock would suffice. There would always be someone to welcome him in.

In the old days, a home almost always had grandparents, parents, and children all living in one house. Someone was always home to open the door. In the modern world, however, most people work or go to school and leave the house empty. When children finish school and return home, parents are still working. Therefore, everyone has to carry keys. And a variety of keys are needed for the house, car, store, office, and bank safety-deposit box.

When I was living in Chicago, I lost one of these important keys—the house key—and accidently locked myself out of the house one evening. I called my son, knowing that he had a spare key to the house, but unfortunately he was out of town at the time on vacation. I felt stuck and frustrated. The sun had set, and it was getting darker. Inside the house were my key, my cell phone, and all the comforts of my home. Suddenly, because of my little mistake, I became homeless. Imagine how I felt when I had to go to my neighborhood Dunkin' Donuts and ask to borrow some change for the public payphone! Luckily, I was able to contact one of my good friends, who invited me to spend the night at her house. The next morning, I was very thankful when my friend's son was able to help me unlock the door to my house.

Over time, I have gradually gained more appreciation for this learning experience. I used to take my keys for granted, thinking they were just tools I needed to enter closed doors. Because of this one key incident, especially after experiencing all the hardship it caused, reentering my house felt like entering heaven. I had never felt such a strong sense of relief, peace, and gratitude before.

Previously, when I heard a church sermon about heaven, I did not take it as seriously as I do now. Like other Christian believers who hope to live in heaven, I was wondering how someone could get a key to heaven. Because of this incident, I started to think deeply about the path there.

Considering how wonderful I felt when reentering my house, I can imagine what a wondrous feeling it will be to enter heaven. People have doors to their hearts, the same kind as the doors to their homes. A person suffering from stress may need help, but if his heart is closed, even the ones closest to him are unable to help. For example, some of my old customers would openly share with me their difficult and stressful moments in their lives. What they needed was an open ear and support. I sympathized with their pain and emotions and prayed for them. When

I heard that their problems were solved, my heart would feel relieved and full of joy. By trusting me, they got the key to open up part of their hearts.

Today, we live in the midst of stress, which causes illness and creates further problems. In times of stress, opening your heart and discussing your concerns with your family, a close friend, mentor, or neighbor will help to bring them together to deal with your stress, and in return their lives will also be blessed. How can I receive the key to heaven? As mentioned in the Bible, I think it is about following the footsteps of Jesus to help and serve others.

In that key accident, I was blessed that I had my lady friend whose heart was open and who was there for me. She is not even my family, yet she took care of me like a younger sister when I was locked out of my home. For that, I am truly grateful. Every now and then I still open my heart and lean on my lady friend for her love and support. I also want to be there for those who are suffering or in pain and open my heart for them to lean on me when situations get tough.

gloria.d.cha@outlook.com

Beauty of One Sip of Coffee
Eun Sil Chung

The rain has been pouring endlessly from the day into the night. It is times like this that I enjoy listening to Chopin's "Nocturne" while sipping a freshly brewed cup of coffee. The combination of these three elements gives me an almost indescribable, deep sense of balance and harmony.

A lot of people gravitate toward the taste of coffee when it rains, and I am certainly not an exception. And tonight this particular cup brings something quite special, something entirely different than the coffee I had at work earlier.

It led me to think back on how I got started with coffee. It started during my high school days, when I consumed it primarily to stay awake and study through many nights.

Back then, I didn't even recognize the aroma of coffee and was far from understanding its depth. I chased coffee in a different way during college, mainly for the atmosphere of coffeehouses and the mood it afforded; I still did not appreciate its depth. Now, in my fifties, coffee has become not only a daily necessity but a pleasurable part of my life—a unique companion during the periods when I am pensive about the meaning of life. After all, isn't it the little things in every day that add up to years and ultimately sum up our lives?

My first coffee in the morning is the most essential one of the day. While consuming that first cup of freshly brewed black coffee, I review the previous day's business and plan for the new day. This routine, as small as it is in a bigger picture of life, can never be taken lightly, and through this first cup I learn some new life lessons too.

Though by the time I'm down to the last few sips my coffee has become cold, I still finish the cup. It has become my way of declaring, albeit only to myself, that I will lead my day the way I intended.

My midday cup often brings a variety of different meanings because of the daily events of people around me as well as their laughter and tears, and these meanings, trivial or not, touch me in a way that allows me to discover my deep love for life.

At the end of the day, I drink a big mug of coffee at my store while looking at all the employees wrapping up another long day and praise them for their hard work and dedication. Their earnest faces reacting to my words reveal the sacredness of labor.

It is nighttime now; everyone is ready to go to bed. Yet here I am brewing another cup of coffee. What kind of meaning is embedded in this last cup? This is the time for not thinking, forgetting, and emptying myself for a state of peace. As such, I find entirely different feeling while drinking this last cup, in contrast with the others at work. In this moment of solitude, without any outside stimulants, I realize life is really worth living; life is beautiful all on its own.

eunsilchung@hotmail.com

The Belly Button
Ki Hoon Kim

Half a century and six years ago, I had a privilege of visiting the three West African nations to take part in their annual international meetings sponsored by the former World University Service (WUS). After WWII, students in American colleges and universities had been donating money and books for their counterparts in developing nations through WUS. This made it possible for the recipients to pursue their studies.

The Korean WUS was formed following the 1953 armistice of the Korean War. The US head office provided enough funds to Korea to buy a large but old house in Seoul, which was converted into a hostel to accommodate seventy college students, about sixty percent of them male. The students came from many colleges and universities in the capital city. During my senior year I became one of those fortunate to live in the hostel at a very reasonable cost.

When I was studying in the United States, the Director of the Korean WUS appointed me to represent Korea at international conferences for three consecutive years, Canada in 1958, West Africa in 1959, and West Germany in 1960. In 1959 I also attended a workshop in Sierra Leone, a work camp in Ghana, and a general assembly held in Nigeria. No one in these countries had ever met a Korean before, and only a few knew where Korea was.

While in Sierra Leone, we stayed at the Forah Bay College dormitory in Freetown. I was assigned to a room with a dozen of other participants. The first night I was awakened by a small lizard that fell on my arm. As I looked up, I was startled to see so many of them crawling on the ceiling! A native student assured me that it was harmless. Nevertheless, I was unable to go back to sleep. Moreover, the humidity was so high that within a few days all of my airmail envelopes were stuck together.

As a result of my first visit to these former British colonies, I learned a lot about them. One memory in particular sticks out in my mind. Most of the children in these three nations shared one common trait: their navels, or belly buttons, were as big as eggs, but round. Perhaps the midwives in the 1950s had no up-to-date knowledge about how to treat newborn babies' umbilical cords at that time, resulting in protruding umbilici. Since then, I became interested in finding diversified cultures related to the navel.

In Japan, when a newborn baby's umbilical cord dropped, the parents preserved it in a small paulownia wooden box. Their language also has some humorous expressions. For example, when they say, "Our navel boils the tea," it does not mean the Japanese have an electric device in the center of their body to prepare hot tea. It simply means, "the story is so hilarious that we roar with laughter." It can also be said as "our navel changes the lodging." Koreans express the same situation by saying, "We are pulling our belly buttons out."

In Japanese, "bending the navel" indicates one is so mad that he refuses to talk. "She is manipulating the navel" applies to housewives who set aside a certain amount of the household budget for out-of-the-ordinary purposes. When the situation is hopeless, they say, "We bite our navels."

Koreans also have their own idioms regarding the belly button. "Adding a mirror made of grinding metal (copper) to the navel" indicates one has a sharp insight that can see another person's mind thoroughly. "The belly button is laughing" means one is dumbfounded. When one is dancing with the belly button exposed, it is "the navel dance." A "navel T" is a T-shirt showing one's belly button. If someone feels hungry, he or she uses "the navel clock" to indicate mealtime is at hand. "The navel is larger than the baby (or belly) itself" shows that subsidiary expenses surpass the original outlay—for example, when shipping postage is more than the price of the merchandise.

Now, the expression also appears in some theological aspects. First, in the Bible, the navel was mentioned twice. One is in Song of Solomon 7:2, "Your navel is rounded goblet which lacks no blended beverage." The other is Ezekiel 16:4, "As for your nativity, on the day you were born your navel cord was not cut." The latter sounds like the African children's navel that I saw in 1959.

Second, we may examine the navels of the first couple,

Adam and Eve. In my personal assumption, they did not have any! This is due to the fact that they were *created*, not physically born as infants. I am sure that their first son, Cain, asked his parents when his curiosity began to show—around the age, say, three or four—about their lack of the navels, although he himself had one. In contrast, masterpiece paintings drawn by world-famous painters actually added the navels to all of their pictures. Michelangelo, for example, who drew the famous ceiling paintings in the Sistine Chapel, "The Creation of Adam," clearly depicted his navel. So was Eve depicted in other pictures. However, I still contend that as God's original creations, Adam and Eve should remain navel-less.

As we know, laughter is the best medicine. In situations of hardship, let's do as the Japanese phrase suggests, "navels boil tea," and the Korean phrase, "pulling our belly buttons out." we should enjoy the best medicine and lead every day in the positive and optimistic way. Everyone should have "the happy navel."

Pennies With a Purpose
Ki Hoon Kim

According to a Korean tradition, when one talks about his own family members he usually tends to be more humble by describing them to be good-for-nothing. Nevertheless, I feel more compelled to boast about my grandson.

My daughter-in-law was working at a children's hospital that provided treatment to long-term pediatric patients. In the fall of 2001, when her son, Yoonho, also known as Andrew, was only three years old, she took him to walk around the hospital. She asked him, "What do you think the children in the hospital would want for Christmas?" She thought he would definitely say presents from their parents. Unexpectedly, he replied, "We have to help them go home for Christmas." Then she asked him again, "Good idea. But what if most of the children have to stay at the hospital for a long time?" His reply surprised her again: "Then I will use all my money to buy a lot of toys, wrap them in beautiful paper, and give them to them, just like their birthday presents." With this, he offered his piggy bank, which contained about $6.50, mostly in pennies.

This reply gave his mom an inspiration to help him launch a noble project. She made all of us, **Andrew**'s entire family, including both sets of his grandparents, agree to engage in a "Pennies with a Purpose" movement to collect as many pennies as possible. Andrew's dad punched slits in the plastic covers of coffee cans to create piggy banks. To begin with, we started to empty our pockets and pulled out every penny for Andrew to put into his can. Hearing the dropping sound of coins brought smiles to all of our faces, especially my grandson. We continued to hunt for coins in every handbag, drawer, bureau top, and forgotten jacket—even under the sofas. Day after day, as the amount of the coins was increasing, my grandson began to shake his can full of coins to everyone and showed his satisfaction. We used to ignore pennies that fell on the ground, but now each coin became precious.

Every one of us felt so good to be engaged in such a worthwhile purpose. With the number of pennies growing, we began to wrap them into copper-colored wrappers, each holding fifty coins.

We all agreed to collect $100 worth of pennies together during the first year, which was 10,000 pennies! Very soon my grandson's project reached beyond our family by word of mouth. The rapid responses came from so many friends, neighbors, church members, Sunday school children, and even strangers. Our goal of $100 was attained within the first month. One church member brought 5,231 pennies, which he had been collecting for many years. A bank in town and a local toy store manager promised that if $50 were collected, they would match the amount. The final sum wound up to be over $1,000, just in time for Christmas!

In October, the *New Britain (CT) Herald* newspaper reported on its front page Andrew's Pennies with a Purpose movement, with a photo of my grandson holding a coffee can full of pennies. So did our local ABC/TV news. In addition, the August 2005 issue of *Hartford Magazine* carried a special article, "Kids Who Care," about six children, three teenagers and three elementary school kids, including my six-year-old grandson as the youngest, who contributed for the betterment of their communities.

In those days, whenever we visited Andrew, it became our joy to bring him pennies. Every time, he shook the can and listened to the sound of coins with a big smile. A friend of mine even took a coffee can together with the local paper article to a popular municipal golf course and solicited voluntary donation. Whenever people played a round of golf, each person donated fifty cents for achieving every par. Many children also took part in the collection of coins by emptying their piggy banks.

Sesame seeds are tiny, and each one alone cannot do anything. Yet, our forefathers collected a lot of them and roasted and pressed them to get delicious sesame seed oil. Yes, these pennies are just like sesame seeds. Each one may be almost useless, but as we collect a lot of them, they can do remarkable things. Indeed, "many a little makes a miracle." First, the collecting process itself gave us all a sense of accomplishment. Secondly, otherwise uncirculated pennies became coins with renewed purpose. Thirdly, we could buy a lot of toys to make many children happy, especially those whose sickness may be incurable.

Finally, on Christmas Day, all who took part in Pennies with a Purpose came to sing carols with the children in the hospital ward and shared a very unforgettable and joyful time together. Each participant learned about the beauty of cooperation and helping others. Indeed, giving is always more blessed than receiving. Above all, this program taught children from early ages many good lessons through participating in a worthy cause.

We are the community of sesame seeds. Together, we can accomplish a lot. This is the joy of Christmas: "Glory to God in the highest, goodwill toward mankind, and peace on earth."

kimk@ccsu.edu

A Happy Life
Min Jung Kim

What is the meaning of happiness?

These days, Korean Americans who visit Korea say after returning that the standard of living has improved a great deal there. However, what I know is that people there may have become well off economically, but fewer people are actually happy. Then what does it mean to have a happy life? I found that it usually occurs to those who are at peace with themselves, those who lead a life with a sense of ease.

About that time of the year when winter reluctantly gave way to spring, I received an invitation to a birthday party from an Irish friend named Barbara. She was turning thirty-nine years old but had no children yet. Last year, when she got pregnant, her husband was ecstatic, but it ended up with a miscarriage. The couple was not depressed by it and still came to our store with smiles. They looked more like brother and sister. They had four cats that they treated like their children.

I couldn't go to the party because my son came back from college, so I asked Barbara if I could stop by her house before the party for a cup of coffee on my way home from work. She accepted delightfully.

Somehow I had this preconceived notion that Barbara

would live like a typical American. Unlike a Korean social gathering, where there is always a table full of carefully prepared cooked food, American parties usually are more casual, with chips and cookies, music, dancing, and lots of conversation. At such gatherings, instead of discussing topics about money and social status as most Koreans do, the guests spend time sharing stories about their daily lives.

It was around eight o'clock when I rang her bell, and none of Barbara's friends had arrived yet. They might come after cleaning up their dinner or taking care of their kids.

From outside, her house looked worn-out like other houses in the neighborhood, but they fixed the house here and there so one could distinguish the worn parts versus the fixed parts right away. As my husband and I drank hot coffee, they showed us around the house and told us that it took them two years to fix it.

This town is a small island that connects Queens and Brooklyn. It once used to be owned by the city, lined with worn-out houses without sewage. But years ago, the land became privately owned, so the price of the houses soared. Soon many people fixed their houses, sold them, and moved away, especially those of Irish descent who were the leaders of the town. Barbara explained that she bought her house before it became privately owned, claiming that it made her lucky.

She showed off her cat. Stroking her fur, she asked me, "Isn't she pretty?" I nodded agreeably, but actually inside I was filled with fear. Big cats quietly jumping out from this and that corner made me nervous.

My husband, who was oblivious to what I was going

through, seemed more fascinated by the handiwork of the house and was listening attentively to what Barbara's husband Dennis was saying.

If it were up to us, we would have hired people for a couple of months to fix our house, but Barbara and Dennis saved and borrowed money to buy theirs, so they learned how to improve the house by themselves. Over a period of two years, they fixed their house with their own hands and derived happiness and pleasure from improving it. To them, fixing their house was like giving birth to a baby, raising the child by breastfeeding and watching the child grow up. It was a source of happiness for them.

Behind the house in the backyard is a pond. During the summer, it provides beautiful scenery for people to admire. Their furniture, kitchenware, and figurines around the house looked ordinary, but we could see they had invested time and care into them, which made their home look like a cozy nursery school in Korea.

Soon their friends started arriving one by one or two at a time with presents wrapped in pretty packages, and my conversation with Barbara ended. She invited us to come over for a barbecue during the summer. We said our good-byes and left.

On my way home, looking up at a bright star in the dark sky, I realized that I was so much moved by this couple. Although they were not well off, they found happiness in building their own home. Happiness is not far away. It is right here inside us and in our neighbors. With this realization, a smile brightened my face. I rushed home with overwhelming joy.

Leftover Space
Min Jung Kim

I started drawing and painting, perhaps because I wanted to feel at ease at the late stage of my life.

I began pursuing fine arts through receiving special instructions and lessons from Mr. Kim, a very well-versed scholar and member of the Korean Literary Society. I paused for some time when my schedule would not allow it, and then picked it up again when I attended a fine arts college in Manhattan.

There are different types of painting, such as Asian or Western painting, etching, and acrylic, but I did not want to draw and paint for the sake of art. I believed that there was more value and meaning in being able to focus on one thing. I was satisfied with being able to draw something with my own hands, instead of aiming to create a masterpiece or leave a legacy in my name. Actually, drawing pictures was more an opportunity for me to closely examine myself.

This early morning, as usual, I rushed out to take the express bus to Manhattan. Suddenly I began to worry about whether I was going to see that man who was always sitting in the same spot right across the street from Carnegie Hall. The man was in his forties, and his ragged clothes gave off less the air and smell of an active artist than a homeless man. Every time I went to school, he was sitting there on the concrete floor as if he had stayed up all night, with the same squatting position as last week and the week before last.

Of course there are many homeless people like him, and luckily it was thirty or forty degrees Fahrenheit; otherwise, he would have frozen to death. I could not understand how he could keep the same posture in the same spot in this ever-changing environment.

We usually hear that we should clear our mind and unclutter what is inside our heart, which will give us a sense of ease that people usually obtain at a mature age, but I often wonder just how much one can clear his or her mind. Maybe when someone cleans up the front porch area, he can brag about how much he or she has emptied his mind. If someone claims to have cleared his mind, is it someone who bolts open the doors of the mind and gets rid of everything, all the way up to the yard, or someone who clears away everything up to the living room and then all the way to the bedroom?

It's problematic for a homeless or transcendental person who has no attachment to worldly possessions and no regrets in life. To them, emptying everything and sitting on the street brings no big difference to their life. It is also problematic for those who are so attached to materialism that only sitting and grinding away at the pavement doesn't really take away anything from them.

One time I read in some magazine about the courage of an American woman who wrote about her experience of getting rid of all of her stuff. She was so obsessed with buying things that whenever she had money, she immediately went out and bought something. But she realized that she had no peace inside. She enjoyed the moment when she bought something, but soon it became a burden. Sometimes she would use something once and never use it again, and at other times she did not even open the package and just neglected the item so that her bedroom and living room became full of these purchased items.

However, one day she made up her mind, and with no exception, she sold all of her stuff at dirt-cheap prices or just gave them away when she was about to move to a different place. When she was finally moving, she got rid of all of her stuff except for her necessary belongings, which she could literally fit into the trunk of her car just as she had planned.

It was then that she felt a sense of freedom. She wrote about these experiences in her debut work, and it became a great hit. When she was interviewed and asked various questions, she said she was enjoying her life.

I thought it would be good for me to clear my mind during this season when the shoots are sprouting up, but then again, I thought it would be better for me to organize everything around the house first.

greenartschool@yahoo.com

The Birdhouse
Myong Soon Kim

Michael, my neighbor across the street, built a pretty birdhouse. Hammering and painting all morning long, he created a beautiful work of art. Michael is an artist from Kuwait and has been in exile here in the United States. The birdhouse certainly shows his artistic talent.

Whenever I open the curtains of my upstairs bedroom windows, I can see the birdhouse standing right in front of me. Its roof is red, the walls are brown, and its pale yellow windows are rimmed with black strips. Both the front and the back of the birdhouse have a window with two small cute holes next to the windows. It even has a tiny chimney the size of a finger. The more I look at it, the lovelier it looks. Whenever I have a little time to pause, I gaze into the birdhouse and get lost in my thoughts. The birdhouse seems to convey Michael's warmth and the loving mind he must have had while building it.

I was very curious as to what kind of bird could live in such a birdhouse, because to me the holes were so small that any kind of bird would have a difficult time getting in and out. Perhaps that is why I haven't seen any birds going into it. Michael put so much care into building the birdhouse, but it just sits there in his garden uselessly, more like an ornament that displays his artistic talent. It seems to conceal its unfulfilled purpose.

Just as the main character Johnsy in O'Henry's "The Last Leaf" established a purposeful connection with the leaves of the tree outside her window, I watched over the birdhouse and kept wishing that a bird, a tiny little bird perhaps, would fly in and claim ownership of it. Sometimes a large bird would fly to it, look through the holes, peck at it a few times, and then fly away. At other times a bird or two would cautiously circle around it and hurriedly leave. The birdhouse was all dressed up and ready to receive its tenant, but no bird would move in. It brought to my mind the image of a beautifully dressed bride from a bygone era who had been jilted by her husband on the first night of their honeymoon.

Maybe tomorrow a bird would finally fly in and lay its eggs. Then, when the eggs are hatched, hopes for the future would continue. I wonder if perhaps we humans attempt to fill our lives by wishing for something other than what is.

Last winter, while looking out of the window and seeing the snow-covered empty birdhouse, I often felt lonesome and wishful, possibly because I tried to suppress my wistful thoughts about the birdhouse. Although the novelty of it had worn off, since I saw it so often, it still looked so beautiful to me that I wished I could make one just like it. Gradually, when I was staring at the birdhouse, what kept coming to my mind was the phrase "good for nothing," in spite of my acknowledgment that it wasn't entirely useless.

At times I would blame Michael's old age, which I believed to be the cause of his poor judgment in making the holes so small that no birds could possibly fly in. I would criticize his lack of common sense that I thought was typical of most artists. So disappointed about the lack of activity in the birdhouse, I withdrew my attachment and became indifferent to it.

One day, the Korean novelist Choi Myung Hee came to visit me at my house. Being very much impressed by the birdhouse, she exclaimed, "Oh my, it's so pretty. It really is. It seems to be standing there just for you, Myong Soon!" She went on to say, "I think he must have built it because he was inspired by your presence, a small pretty Asian woman going about the house."

Before hearing Choi's rather imaginative exclamation and the way this novelist felt about the birdhouse, it never occurred to me that Michael's creation had anything to do with me. I just liked the fact that the birdhouse was standing there where I could see it. But as I was listening to her interpretation, I was instantly convinced that she was right, so I responded, "Oh, yes, you are right. That birdhouse is there for me," as if I really understood Michael's true intention. I then realized how miraculously my previous criticism and negativity about Michael's imperfect creativity was replaced with a feeling of joy.

Spring arrived, and I saw Michael repainting the birdhouse. I called out, "Michael! Michael!" and showered him with compliments about the birdhouse. I told him, "Michael, you have no idea what pleasure I get from watching your birdhouse. I want you to know how much

I love it. But I'm afraid that the holes are too small, and that is why not even one bird could fly in. Why don't you make them a little larger?"

Then he said, "Oh, no, Robin, these holes ought to be exactly one-and-a-half inches. If they were any bigger than that, the larger birds would get in and eat the sparrows that live there. The eggs are in there now."

"Oh, I see," I responded. I didn't know that the birdhouse was safely holding treasures that could be exchanged with nothing else. How ignorant I was to assume that there was nothing inside, just by seeing it from the outside only. Deeply occupied with this thought, I kept staring at the birdhouse. I had quite a different feeling toward it now than before. It seemed more reliable. I could imagine a bird, a symbol of my relief and joy, flying out from it and into my arms. It opened my mind's eye, which had been previously shut. I could feel a ray of hope shining through me, deepening and widening my inner wisdom.

I was not aware that the sparrows had already moved in, but I was very glad that they now had a safe place to hatch their eggs. Realizing that Michael's love and concern for these small and helpless creatures motivated him to create such a birdhouse, I felt I was as close to him as to it.

I told him, "Thank you, Michael. The birdhouse has been a wonderful gift for me. Had it not been for the birdhouse, my life in this new neighborhood would have been boring and lonesome. I hope that the sparrows will hatch their eggs soon. I would love to see the baby birds."

Michael responded, "Robin, thank you for understanding."

I could see Michael's wrinkled face brightening up in the warm spring sunlight. The thought that Michael and I might develop a wonderful friendship through the birdhouse passed over me.

Valentine's Day
Myong Soon Kim

Tomorrow is Valentine's Day, a day to honor the love that we share with each other. I feel so happy to go to the store to buy three boxes of chocolates with red heart-shaped chocolates in each. Being loved is a wonderful thing, but being able to love someone is even more beautiful. It is said that loving and expressing love need to be practiced, and I am grateful to have a family where I can plant my pure love into the soil that cultivates our relationships.

Ordinarily, I have difficulty saying "I love you" to my husband and two children, Hae Rin and Young Woo. When I was growing up, it wasn't customary to verbalize one's feelings of affection, and therefore it is difficult for me to tell my family how much I love them. For this reason, I am thankful that we have Valentine's Day, which encourages and allows me to express my true, time-tested love to my family and offer them a token of my love. I believe that receiving a Valentine's Day card with the red heart and a rose symbolizing love makes one feel very much loved.

Displayed on my desk is a Valentine's Day card that I received from a friend who is a poet. It has on it a picture of three smiling hearts, along with the following words that she wrote.

> I applaud you silently for your wonderful writing
> And the way you so meaningfully weave your life.
> Let's get together for a cup of flowery and
> fragrant tea.
> On this Valentine's Day that is overflowing with affection,
> I send you my faint expression of love.

The more I read her card, the more heart palpitations I feel her words bring to my breast. I deeply feel her friendship, her modesty, and kindness keep me refreshed and welcomed, like the way I feel when looking up at the stars on a clear night. Our lives are in such a hustle that she and I haven't had a chance to get together and converse to our heart's content; nevertheless, our friendship has continued as we walk together along the stepping-stones of life.

Every human being experiences loneliness and a feeling of separation at times, without exception. However, because we receive love from our parents, lovers, spouses, and friends and live in a sea filled with love, we laugh or we cry. Even in our fast-paced and materialistic society, love makes us all human. But if we focus on receiving love rather than giving love, then selfish egotism will wound our loving hearts.

"Mommy, I love you! I love you!" my children tell me. Although I may reply by saying, "Anyone can repeat that phrase. I would like it better when you show me your love through your actions, like emptying the garbage and studying diligently," it makes me happy to hear those words from my children.

Last summer, we had eight middle school children from Korea who were visiting the United States stay with us at our house for a couple of weeks. The students all called me on New Year's Day from Korea to tell me that they loved me, and naturally I told them that I loved them as well. How delightful they were! It has been quite a while since I received their calls, but those loving words of the students still ring in my ears and make me very happy.

Recently I read an article in a magazine about Valentine's Day. The title was "The day that a woman can initiate the celebration of love." The title implies that it is the man who usually takes the first act on showing love, and on this day it is okay for a woman to remind her loved ones of the significance of their love. I find it pleasurable to just send a lighthearted Valentine's Day card and a rose rather than making the expression of love too serious and burdensome.

myongskim@hotmail.com

Finding Miss Beefus
Oak Soo Kim

It was a late autumn afternoon, a few days before Thanksgiving, when an unfamiliar number tagged "KS" flashed on my telephone. For a few seconds I hesitated before grabbing the phone, hoping it was not another telemarketing call. I thought to myself, *What is this Kansas caller going to sell me now?* With some reluctance, I mumbled, "Hello?"

"This is Kathy Beefus."

I didn't really catch the caller's name. I replied, "Pardon me?"

"Kathy Beefus. I understand that you've been looking for me?"

I became suddenly wide awake. I was holding the phone so tightly that my body was almost shivering with shock, and my voice broke. "Yes, yes! Wow, yes! Are you really Miss Beefus?" While I spoke, my mind raced. *Oh, no. I should not cry. Soo Kim, please calm down and talk to her.* "Oh, my God! You are still around!" This may sound a bit inappropriate, as if I was not expecting her to live this long, but I truly did not have high hopes that I would be able to find her after we parted a half century ago in 1965.

We briefly talked about our families—our husbands,

our children, our grandchildren. I joked about how I was her student a long time ago, but now that young girl was a grandma with her gray hair dyed black. I was so thankful that she was still healthy enough to meet us if we could make a trip to Canton, Kansas, someday in the future. I told her that I had been looking for her for over a year because our class—her former thirty students, most of us seventy years old—was planning to host a special reunion this year and wanted to invite her to the event.

Looking back on my efforts to find Miss Beefus, I voluntarily appointed myself to lead the search, though I hadn't any clue from the beginning. I contacted the Presbytery of New York as a first step, asking if they could help me find a missionary teacher to South Korea in the period of 1963 to 1966. After several weeks of waiting, my inquiry was transferred to the Kansas Presbytery. About three or four months had gone by with countless e-mail exchanges, in the end, they did not find any record that dated that far back.

A few months passed without any further result, so I started to call a couple of her friends from the old days. They told me they had lost contact with her more than twenty years ago.

Therefore, I turned to the almighty Google, typing in her maiden name. If she had gotten married, my luck rested on this half of her name. The website gave me a few names with the city or town attached, but I didn't have a clue of her whereabouts. Not to mention, the site also asked for a membership fee of about $9.00 per month. The idea of monthly payment ticked me off. I would prefer a one-time payment for the service. Two days later, I got an e-mail telling me my monthly premium went down to $2.99 per month.

In early October, I decided to call the City Hall of Wichita, Kansas, for some unknown reason. The lady who answered the phone was kind and patient with me, and after listening to my search story, she became exceptionally helpful. She gave me a cell phone number of a retired nurse who was a friend of hers. Her friend told me to call the Kansas State Board of Nursing (KSBN). The next day I called the KSBN and received more detailed steps on how to find her. I was so excited at this faint hope of finding her.

I wrote a personal letter about the reason I was looking for Miss Beefus and included my detailed contact information. Although the Kansas Board didn't ask for it, I also enclosed an old discolored picture of her with me. I stuck on the stamp and mailed it in a hurry. Along with the letter, I also sent another message, one that didn't require a stamp. I sent a prayer asking that Miss Beefus would be alive and well somewhere in the state.

Fifty-plus years had passed since she entered our classroom. She was young, tall, slim, and blonde, with two blue eyes as deep as the October sky in Korea. With the help of an interpreter, she was going to teach us about "nursing art." She was soft-spoken but energetic and enthusiastic in her teaching. She seemed very eager to pass her knowledge on to us. She motivated me to study harder.

Not long after her arrival to Daegu, Korea, she came

down with acute hepatitis A, which so commonly infected Westerners. With the poor water quality, she could not possibly have avoided this ailment. Even now, half a century later, I remember her faint blue eyes shaded with jaundice. I felt sorry but thankful that although she was going through such a hard time, she still tried selflessly to fulfill the goodness of the Mission works.

How could I not be so shocked when I finally heard her voice over the phone?

Miss Beefus recently sent me a neat handwritten letter with a beautiful picture of her family—her daughter, her Korean son-in-law (what a small world!), her most adorable five granddaughters, her handsome and healthy-looking husband, and finally my teacher, who has aged so gracefully and is in good health. She looks the same! I could have recognized her if we passed each other on the street, with her short haircut and not an ounce of extra fat anywhere. Just like in 1963! In less than a week's time, half of my class got her photo through my e-mail.

I am so happy and grateful that we will be able to reflect on our younger days together and that I am able to say a long-overdue thank you to our wonderful teacher.

oaksookim@gmail.com

Shakespeare in the Park
Chune Hee Lee

"King Lear visits the heart of Manhattan in Central Park. John Lithgow stars as the mad king." The *New York Times* article stirred me. It reminded me of the pleasure I had in my younger years when going to the theater to watch great plays. Suddenly I got filled with nostalgia for those impassioned times. I was like Marcel Proust, who smelled a cookie and couldn't stop the pouring memory. Theater provoked the young and restless years of my life in Korea. I missed going to plays after I came to America.

It was a pleasant hot summer day in August. The golden sunlight was sparkling on the trees, and the flowers were blooming everywhere. My husband and I woke up at six o'clock in the morning in our New York City apartment and hurried to the Delacorte Theater in Central Park. The ticket line was already long. More people scattered among the trees and beside the water. Looking out at the view, it was as if I was appreciating a Monet landscape.

The tickets were free, so getting them was not easy. You had to wait patiently all the way after you got in the line at daybreak, or even earlier. People have been known to camp out at the park entrance closest to the theater, at

Eighty-First Street and Central Park West, to get the free tickets for that day's performance.

While waiting in line, we saw people bringing all kinds of things to kill the long waiting time. Many of them brought magazines, games, and picnic blankets. A mother and daughter who were the first two on the line brought sleeping bags and had obviously slept overnight right outside the park. I could feel their energy and their love of theater.

The majority of the crowd in line was young people. Much later I realized there was a separate line for seniors. When we were in the seniors' line three days later, I saw they all seemed to be healthier than average, instead of what the stereotype of older people. The lady in front of us, in her midsixties, brought a folding chair and a book. She said that Shakespeare in the Park is one of her favorite things to do in the summer, and she came back every year. The lady at the end of the line complained that the man in front of her was taking up too much space. But they later became friends. Everybody was laughing and had a pleasant time. *As we get older, we are like kids again, I thought.*

The deli nearby took breakfast orders for people waiting in line. One young woman who was wearing a bicycle helmet appeared with breakfast for her husband, who looked old enough to be her father. We all thought she was another delivery person. That scene was so unique but delightful. There was a man who played the flute. Listening to music in Central Park on a spectacular summer day was an unexpected surprise for me. Despite the overcrowded park and a hot day in New York City, the Shakespeare festival made it worthwhile.

My love of theater was instilled in me by my father. I watched the play that he produced when I was in a junior high school. I still remembered the day, more than forty years ago, when I excitedly watched Goethe's *Faust* with my father at the National Theater in Seoul, Korea. At intermission, my father usually took me backstage and introduced me to the leading actor. I could never forget that thrilling moment. It was my favorite memory related to theater.

When I met my husband for the very first time, we spent most of our time talking about theater. He had acted as a main character in a play while he was in college. When he said that woman couldn't produce theater, I was really upset about his biased view, but that joke turned out to be a nice icebreaker between us.

I was particularly interested in the plays by Eugene O'Neill and Tennessee Williams. I drowned myself in *Desire under the Elms*, *The Glass Menagerie*, and *The Night of the Iguana*. I longed to play a part in one of those plays. Living someone else's life on the stage was so fascinating to me in those years.

I had never seen Shakespeare's *King Lear* performed on stage before. It started as such a lovely evening. The Delacorte Theater is an open-air amphitheater with 1,800 seats. I looked around at the audience. The mood was very festive. They were all excited and delighted, feeling lucky to be there. So was I.

The story begins when King Lear decides to divide

his kingdom among his three daughters and rejects his favorite daughter, Cordelia. She stands silent when asked how much she loves him. I could feel how much Lear craved his daughter's love. King Lear's loneliness and sorrow pierced my heart. It made me think about my mother. I realized how lonely she was, living alone for over thirty years after my father passed away. Now as an aging parent myself, I still secretly harbor the foolish hopes and dreams to keep my children beside me all my life.

The scene of Lear's awakening moment of compassion on the heath was impressive. It was particularly heartbreaking to see the last scene, when King Lear holds the dead body of his beloved daughter, Cordelia, and cries with such painful grief. In that tragic moment the entire audience remained extremely quiet and fully immersed in the sorrow with him. King Lear's greatest war was the battle he won with himself.

Because it was an outdoor performance with street noise, I couldn't hear every line, but I was happy to be there and had a sense of accomplishment. Whatever the critics' comments were about the play, I was moved.

The Shakespeare festival was originally conceived by Joseph Papp in 1954. Papp began with a series of Shakespeare workshops and then moved on to free productions on the Lower East Side. Eventually, the plays moved to a lawn in front of Turtle Pond in Central Park. He wanted to reach audiences who might never have seen a play before and who were unable or unwilling to pay. One person's impossible dream made it possible for me to dream again at this later age. What a wonderful feeling!

Can you imagine me sitting out on a summer night in Central Park in the middle of New York City, watching a Shakespeare play that was so amazing and absolutely free? What a cheerful and energetic place to live! I feel so blessed living in New York. My heart was filled with so much delight and excitement that it almost burst. It was one of the most magical nights I've ever had in the theater.

The Liberation of Growing Old
Chune Hee Lee

My vision has been getting blurry these days. I checked with my eye doctor, and he told me that my eyesight would get dim as time went by. His recommendation was to wear eyeglasses. It made me sad. "Don't worry. This is part of the aging process, but you have most beautiful eyes at your age," he tried to comfort me. Frankly, it had not crossed my mind until then that I was getting older, even though I never thought I would be immortal. I had an overwhelming pressure to make a living, maintain my career, and raise my children. I was preoccupied with my busy schedule. Aging befell me all of a sudden. It was a cold December day. The unexpected news froze not only my body but also my mind.

In ancient times, people notoriously mistreated their elderly parents, who were unable to work and still needed care. While that has changed dramatically, older people are still viewed negatively by society. I witnessed that myself while I was working in a nursing home. Older people were truly helpless, dependent, sick, isolated, senile, and depressed. Older people are often thought of as burden and problem. It is an ugly picture.

People used to describe the older population with

the words such as "senile," "frail," "institutionalized," " homebound," "vulnerable," and "dependent," and bedridden elderly have even more undesirable implications. I was very unhappy to hear those demeaning words—not to mention that most elderly people are easily affected by what they hear and read.

One day I went out with my daughter to the department store. I asked questions about certain merchandise to the sales clerk, and he answered to my daughter instead of to me. How humiliated I felt! Older people usually become invisible when younger people are around. Why do people have such punitive attitudes toward old people?

According to a *New York Times* article, when a large sample of twenty- to twenty-nine-year-old people were examined by a team based at the Yale School of Public Health, the result showed three-quarters of them were found to deprecate old people. As much as a third of them advocated banning old people from public activities like shopping. It tells us that age is our defining characteristic, so we will become nothing when getting old. Aging is not a disease, but a condition upon which we have been given life.

Betty Friedan, in her book *The Fountain of Age*, argued that seeing age only as decline from youth makes age itself the problem. Age alone cannot define who we really are. We can be defined by what we have become. Older people are thrilled to hear that they look younger than their age. They dress like adolescents. They remove their wrinkles with plastic surgery. They want to stay young as long as they can. How long, and how well, can we really live by trying to bypass the aging trap? We ultimately create a stereotype of the helpless elderly. Why are we not looking at age as a new, evolving stage of human life? The author stresses that our drive for continued involvement in life is denied by the problem of age mystique.

After my two children left for college, I wondered whether life would make me happy again. I have had times of struggle, emptiness, and longing. For myself, I do fear being a sick and helpless old person. At age fifty, I registered to continue study at a neighboring university. After three and a half years, I got a master's degree in gerontology. As soon as I graduated, I had a chance to work at an assisted living facility. While I was working there I experienced the elderly's vulnerabilities and agonies and have more compassion toward older people.

When I really accepted the fact that life was really limited, everything within its boundaries became more meaningful and precious for me. Therefore, I tried to focus on living as meaningfully as possible. After we retired, my husband and I were more able to savor life. Now we work in the garden to plant trees, open a vegetable plot, and build a birdhouse. When fall begins, we sweep the fallen leaves on the lawn, trim the trees, and contemplate the beautiful autumn. In the evening we read books and go to movies and watch game shows. We travel to many places and meet all kinds of different people. We talk about our children and grandchildren and thank God for them. What a wonderfully relaxing feeling it is to live every single day. I don't miss any of the stressful days in my younger life.

It is not sad at all to grow old when looking carefully at how the seasons change, with spring, summer, autumn, and winter rotating naturally and beautifully. The liberating attitude of nature educates us: It is not about aging. It is about living.

"Grow old along with me! The best is yet to be." Robert Browning's beautiful poem invites us to challenge and eagerly greet the future. He acknowledges that youth lacks insight into life, but being old is where the best of life is realized.

Now it is early spring. I am looking through my bedroom window, blue sky, bright sunshine, and purple flowers of rhododendrons. They appear so amazingly beautiful, as if I have never seen them before. Will Miranda's new world in Shakespeare's play look like this? My physical eyesight is getting blurred as I get older, but I can see better through my mind's eye.

Aging can be a gift.

monicachunelee@gmail.com

Whispering Walls
Hea Sook Lim

Once in a while, I dream I am being tightly enveloped in someone's embrace. I don't know who that person is, or if I'm hugging them or they are hugging me, but I somehow feel happy when I awake. It gives me a warm feeling, as if the chill in my heart is melting away. They say hugging is the most treasured cure in the world. Just two hands wrapped around the shoulders can melt away the loneliness and solitude built up over years.

It was winter. Winter break was drawing near at the Manhattan Korean School, where I worked briefly. At a fundraising event for the school, different events were auctioned off. One item, skating with students at the Central Park ice rink, was auctioned off at $250. The music teacher and I were in charge of this outing. When the date arrived, we took the children to the ice rink. It was particularly cold and windy on that day, which made it even drearier.

"I'll take the children on the ice to skate. You should stay here and watch and have some coffee."

The younger music teacher was considerate. I bought a sweet hot chocolate instead of coffee and sat on an empty bench. The exciting music and the children happily skating away seemed worlds away from me. Suddenly, someone wrapped his hands around my shoulders and tapped me lightly.

"Thank you for all your hard work in this cold weather!" It was one of the children's fathers.

Was it the cold or my overbearing loneliness? My eyes welled up with tears at this person's touch. I didn't forget this warmth for a long time. I realized for the first time that someone's hand, even with just a slight touch or pat, had the ability to melt someone's heart.

Not long ago, there was a poster exhibition about hands at the Museum of Modern Art. From World War I posters to 1980s Japanese Shiseido ads for nail enamel, the exhibit depicted a wide range of use for hands and what hands symbolize. There were a lot of valuable posters that drew my attention: hands working together to construct a new postwar society, hands typing up a telegram to deliver good news, and hands reading braille, which is nothing short of eyes reading print. In the rough but vivid images of hands, I felt a new gratitude for them.

In contrast, there were also images implying the destructive use of hands: a criminal's hands grasping someone's neck, a fistfight showing conflict, and a thumbs-down motion used to belittle someone else.

Of all the posters, I was most struck by Marek Mosinski's black-and-white "Whispering Walls (Szepczace Sciany)," which portrays a pair of worn-out and old hands. It reminded me of the old film about an old, lonely, and poor delusional widow titled *The*

Whisperers. The large rough hands in the poster filled up the entire image.

What are these hands whispering to us? I wondered. Are they saying that though we try to seize wealth and fame, all that's left in the end is a pair of old and empty hands?

We can use our hands in thousands of different ways in our everyday lives. They can grab, hold, touch, take, or hit. "How am I using *my* hands?" I felt as if my hands were asking me. Am I holding them open greedily to grab more than what I have? Am I clutching my hands together tight in fear of losing the things I have in them? Do I have long nails to scratch other people's hearts?

In some ways, the most beautiful thing our hands can do is hold others'. To hold others' hands, we must set down what we have in them to empty them first. I wish my hands could melt away someone's loneliness and sorrow as those hands did in that tiresome and lonely winter.

Letters Sent in Winter
Hea Sook Lim

The winter light is cold. Somehow, I feel like writing a letter in these chilly winter days. Handwritten letters have been a thing of the past for some time. But as I think of everyone I would send letters to while I choose a card for each one, my mind flutters with excitement like I am a young girl again.

I choose a bright gold card with a picture of an armful of various kinds of fruit for my friend who enthusiastically welcomed me with a get-together when I visited Seoul last year. A friend from my high school days, she is now almost blind because of macular degeneration in one eye and is also receiving treatment in the other. She used to hold on to my arm tight as she carefully walked the bumpy Sejongno alleys. When I think of her adjusting to the fear of permanently losing her sight "with optimism and laughter," I feel twinges of sadness that pains me as if icy waves are washing over my heart.

For my senior colleague, whom I am reminded of whenever I hear the song "Violet," I choose a picture of a pretty girl laboriously propping up with her hands a large rock that's about to fall. My colleague gave me strength and companionship whenever I felt discouraged during my belated academic career. I remember he was happy when he finally found his calling at the end of a long search. However, he tells me that reality is always catching up with him. I feel it's my turn to offer him words of comfort.

As I look through the greeting cards, I am reminded of my father, perhaps because the anniversary of his death is in the winter. I also thought of an old letter my "trendy" father wrote to me, which he called "words sent to a young person." He had crammed his sentences onto a double-sided lined paper in pen as he comforted my broken heart. I remember crying my heart out when I received his letter overflowing with a generous attitude toward life and compassion for his daughter. The longing for my father remains as a postscript never sent.

In my younger days, letters were messengers that brought us romance and longing. We sent love letters, thinking the words "I love you" were immature. We regarded ending a relationship as an act that hurt one's pride, so we would send farewell poems instead. The letters we sent and received contained the sad, joyous, and heartfelt stories in our lives. That is probably why I still hold on to letters more than forty years old.

The winter night is cold. That I have someone to send letters to on this cold and long winter night is a happy thing.

celiz2@naver.com

Our Lifelong Search for Fun
Jung Kil Na

When children are bored, they play with their toys. When they get bored with their toys, they search for new toys. Therefore, parents are always busy replacing the old toys with brand-new ones, and in a short time, the playroom will be filled with a lot of toys. Children keep looking for new toys that will have more movements or produce cooler sounds. Our lives begin with play, and then we constantly search for better ways to pass our time.

When kids get older, their yearning for play enters an even broader field. For some of them, video games, sports, movies, or other electronic devices may occupy their time, while studying and normal daily activities are often pushed to the backseat. When these kids become adults, they tend to put off their work and become addicted to games. Their lives will eventually fall into failure.

Gradually, kids become more interested in social interactions. Some kids who cannot make friends and unable to fit in may spend the rest of their lives with low self-esteem and become loners in society.

The lives of young adults are more occupied with friends and relationships. This is a crucial point in their lives. Any unhealthy, meaningless, or hurtful social interactions may lead to wrong decisions, which may eventually bring despair to life.

Some people start smoking to feel occupied in times of boredom. Others turn to drinking or doing illegal drugs as a way to pass boring times. We know big casinos never lose. A playful start on gambling may lead to habitual play. Once it develops into addiction, no one can escape from it. Many people still go back in hopes of winning a big jackpot yet end up losing everything. The gambling nature of human beings has led to numerous tragedies.

How we spend our youth determines different life paths in our later years. For people who are always pursuing fun, their old age may become more boring and lonely. In our youth, those who work hard can achieve the golden years later.

Of course, life should not be constant work and study. We need quality time to rest our bodies and souls. Life needs good balance.

The most "boring" part of our lives may be the senior years. We are no longer as active as before. We live apart from our families and friends. With little in our possession, we stare at the wall worrying about how we should kill our time each day. To have meaningful golden years, it is important to have healthy hobbies. Reading, going to the movies, traveling, gardening, and volunteering can be some of the activities.

We lead our lives in constant search of fun, and we would never go without it.

jungkilna@yahoo.com

Locking Eyes with Columbus
Ryo Noh

There I was, grazing my hand along the robe of Christopher Columbus.

My children had suggested that for my birthday we meet for dinner in Manhattan. That sounded like any other birthday; shouldn't we do something special? That's what I wanted to say, at least.

I didn't need a banquet in my honor, but it felt like my sixty years, which had passed in ebbs and flows like wind and waves, should be marked with something special. And they were, because I met Columbus.

While New York City was celebrating the 120th anniversary of its Columbus statue, I celebrated my own milestone.

The southwest corner of Central Park is known as Columbus Circle because of this statue. Even Mayor Michael Bloomberg, who lived in New York for five decades, confessed that he had rarely ever looked up at it. Most New Yorkers would probably say the same thing. In the countless times that I passed through the busy intersection, I never felt the urge to stop and consider the figure in the middle. I just lumped it in with all the other statues around the city.

This statue that so many people ignored became the subject of sudden interest because of Tatsu Nishi, the Japanese artist who created the installation called "Discovering Columbus."

After standing high for more than a hundred years—in the snow, rain, and wind—Mr. Columbus for the first time found himself in a warm home, a cozy living room. Once lonely atop his towering column, he was now being continuously sought out by visitors. Even after purchasing our tickets online, we had to endure a long, snaking line before climbing the temporary stairs and entering the room Nishi had built.

With a coffee table covered in magazines, a plush sofa, and a television set, it was like any other American living room. But in the center of it stood Columbus, enormous and proud—a truly extraordinary sight.

Paying no attention to the people crowding his room, Columbus stared into the distance. *Can you see the land on the far end of ocean?* As I approached closer, I noticed the sharp gaze of his eyes puncturing his concrete expression.

Those eyes discovered America.

Columbus landed on these shores in 1492. Almost five hundred years later, in 1982, I landed in New York. In 1952, sixty years after the statue of Columbus was erected, I was born, and today, exactly sixty years later, I was standing in front of him.

When I rested my hand on his robe, I sensed through my fingers that this was a new land for us both. And, in a way, it was thanks to him that I was able to be here. Because I was born in the same season as Columbus Day,

I was able to view this exhibition on my birthday. Nishi, it turned out, was the same age as me.

These connections felt predestined.

After descending the stairs, we walked across the street to have dinner at an Italian restaurant inside the Time Warner Center. Sitting there, we could still see the lights in Columbus' living room outside. It felt grander than receiving bows at a traditional banquet table.

To me, Columbus is no longer just a gray statue. He and I are now acquaintances. Though I doubt I will look into his piercing eyes again, we will always be connected. Now, whenever I pass through Columbus Circle, I lift my eyes to see him. He is still staring at the land on the far end of the ocean. *What are you looking for? If not for you, would I be here now?*

I look up with a glint in my eye.

nohryo@gmail.com

Open House
Jung Sook Yang

Three weeks ago I put my home of twenty years on the market. Today is the open house. It is common for houses on the same block to resemble each other. While they may seem identical from the sidewalk, I believe each house takes on the personality of its inhabitants.

The purpose of an open house is to make the property known to potential buyers, real estate agents, neighbors, and the public. To viewers, it is a carefree event. For the owner, it requires painstaking preparation, after which she has to entrust everything to the hands of the listing agent.

Choosing a home for one's family is similar to going on a blind date. People who attend an open house have an internal checklist that includes size, sturdiness, attractiveness, and other preferences. Most people have very personal and unspoken desires when it comes to choosing a house.

Timing is an important selling point, and most realtors recommend selling in the spring. Just as important, according to my realtor, was staking a big sign in the front yard. But I dragged my feet on both. I felt a detached anxiety very similar to what I felt the night before my daughter's wedding. The house had been an integral part of my family's emotional life for over two decades. I must have developed a strong attachment to it.

I remember feeling vaguely guilty the nights I came home from work to see the house sitting there, dark and uninhabited among the illuminated and lively houses of the neighborhood. It reminded me of a timid child whining at his mother for coming home late everyday.

All my children have grown up and moved out. My mother-in-law, who used to tend a vegetable garden in a corner of the backyard with her grandchildren, also moved out a few years ago.

Right next to the house, an artifact of the stone Buddha practicing Zen meditation is on a table as a guardian over my mother-in-law's room as if it is replacing my mother-in-law's presence. I was reluctant to show the house to strangers—the potential buyers—because of my mother-in-law's stone statue.

As all humans are unique in their own ways, people have different ways of interpreting the things they see. I could see many buyers' personalities in their comments and perspectives on the house. Some people saw different aspects of the house in an optimistic point of view, such as a potential room for the improvement. Looking at the stone Buddha statue, some potential buyers elaborated on the superiority and characteristics of their own religion, while some enjoyed the moment of silence to reflect on their inner mind.

Like the saying "Every Jack has his Jill," my house will meet its new owner. I wish for a loving family who will enjoy happiness, dreams, and joyous moments as my family has had over the years. This house, like a bride preparing for her wedding day, will eventually find the good-natured family who will build a happy future in this cherished property that I have called home for the last twenty years.

New Family
Jung Sook Yang

My daughter e-mailed me photos again today. They are filled with adorable images of her cherished little rascals: Momo, Milky, and Congee. They've grown so fast in just a few weeks.

I hear others speak of their grandchildren, the apples of their eyes—they talk about how much the children enchant them. But my husband and I get to see photos of cats my daughter sends from time to time, as if they are to take the place of grandchildren we might have had.

A year ago my son-in-law's company merged with another large firm in San Jose. He and my daughter prepared to relocate, first finding a place to live there. During this busy time, something unexpected occurred. Someone left five newborn kittens in a box near the entrance where my daughter worked. Being softhearted, my daughter was unable to pass them up and brought two of them home with her. My son-in-law was bewildered but agreed to raise them, agreeing that the kittens, living under the same roof as him and my daughter, were now part of the family.

Despite my daughter and son-in-law's utmost care, the kittens, never breastfed by their mother, were often sick. Visits to the vet were frequent. Once, when the kittens' conditions had, for reasons unknown, worsened to a troubling level, they were moved to a family-run veterinary hospital my daughter found after asking around. The hospital housed three generations of vets. My daughter and son-in-law spent no small sum of money they had set aside for moving to a new house to pay for the kittens' treatments.

My husband does not even like going near cats. When we first immigrated, he suffered from stubborn sores caused by cat fleas that refused to heal. But my daughter and son-in-law liked to socialize and were not at home frequently, so the young kittens became solely our responsibility. We each held one in our hands and fed them every four hours; we patted their backs and burped them. Afterward, they would fall asleep in our hands as if they were in their mother's bosom. Young kittens are unable to control their urination or have a bowel movement on their own—they have to be stimulated. This, too, we also did in the way instructed by my daughter. We rubbed their anal areas with wet paper towels until the cats were ready, at which point they would go to the litter box and do their business. Once finished, they buried their waste with the litter. Though he is much older, Congee sometimes acted out of jealousy, as if he felt hostile toward the new kittens. He often went into the kittens' litter box and dug up the litter, making a mess. When Congee bothered the kittens with his violent acts, they would lower their bodies in defense. Momo and Milky can be quick and smart.

We visited our daughter's house for few days to feed them, clean up after them, and put them to bed. As we took an interest in each of their actions, somehow we became attached to them. My husband would poke their sleeping bodies. When they were awake, they would always try to be cuddled. We even told our daughter to leave one behind.

The trip to San Francisco, delayed ten days because of the kittens, was now approaching. Another problem arose in the process of purchasing plane tickets. Only one pet per person was allowed, so another person had to accompany them to San Francisco.

October was a busy month for me, so I told my daughter I couldn't go with her. My daughter, who never behaved coyly, clung to me and told me she needed my help and that I support her more than anyone else. She went on and on about making it a trip to "see San Francisco" so as to persuade me. I finally gave in—I became a victim.

A hundred dollars was paid for each cat: Momo, Milky, and Congee. On the day we left New York, each cat was placed in a cozy carrier. In the cabin, we carefully held them in our laps as if we were escorting sacred urns. Though it was impossible for the cats to understand anything, my daughter and son-in-law talked to the kittens to soothe them. They only paid attention to the kittens during the slightly boring and uncomfortable six-hour flight.

My daughter e-mailed me photos of them again today.

The members of my daughter's family are smart and quick animals—they understand their owners and try to express themselves by talking through bodily gestures. I feel as if I am looking into my daughter's innocent soul in these photos of the rascals' lives. She has fallen into a one-sided love.

jsyang279@gmail.com

Carnival in Brazil
Bong Won Yeon

The word *Brazil* may evoke thoughts of soccer, samba, and Carnival. Carnival is an annual festival that begins forty days before Lent, usually in the middle of February or early March, depending on what day Easter is celebrated. Carnival always begins on a Friday and is followed by the pinnacle on Tuesday, and the finale on Wednesday. During Carnival, everyone sleeps late, and most offices and shops open in the afternoon on Wednesday.

Based on the lifestyle exhibited during Carnival, some casual observers may thoughtlessly comment that Brazilians are inherently indolent. I would strongly argue that this is a totally incorrect conclusion. In reality, the United States observes more holidays than Brazil. As a result of this, the average US workers work fewer days compared with their Brazilian counterparts. Also, the Brazilian workday for office workers, shopkeepers, and factory workers begins at 7:00 a.m., and Brazil is the only South American country that has no siesta—a short sleep taken at midday until afternoon in hot countries.

Many countries have Carnival, but Brazil's is the most famous because of the 1950s French film *Black Orpheus,* which won the Palme d'Or at the 1959 Cannes Film

Festival. The movie is a modern adaptation of a story from Greek mythology and is set in Rio de Janeiro, one of the most beautiful and recognizable port cities in the world.

The origin of Carnival can be traced to an ancient Egyptian festival. In the early spring, the ancient Greeks paid annual tribute to Dionysus, the god of wine, by dancing frantically. The Roman Empire, successors of the ancient Greek culture, transformed Dionysus into their wine god, Bacchus. They named their festival Carnival and celebrated it with increased extravagance and exuberance. Even after the fall of the Roman Empire, this tradition carried on in many European countries. A new tradition gained popularity when the commoners took to wearing masks during Carnival celebrations. The commoners took part in singing, dancing, and satirically mocking the nobles, monks, and other elite social groups. In response to such effrontery, authorities in governments and churches made many attempts to ban the celebration of Carnival. However, the more they tried, the more Carnival expanded to other countries. In northern Italy, something call the Carnival Cathedral even emerged. Carnival was embraced equally among the common people in Europe because it celebrated their joy and sorrow.

The period and festivities are slightly different from country to country. For example, in Copenhagen, Denmark, the celebration begins on Easter Eve. In Cologne and Munich in Germany, people eat and drink beer all night to celebrate the Beef Evening (Fastnacht) to chase away the winter god. The Nice Carnival is famous in France, and in Italy, Carnival is celebrated as Venice's Mask Ball.

Carnival festivities expanded dramatically into a worldwide phenomenon when European countries colonized many countries in New World. In the Caribbean countries, Carnival was imported by the Spaniards. And later, the Carnival celebration became very famous in Quebec. When Quebec became an English possession, the French inhabitants moved their Cajun culture to Louisiana and transformed Carnival into Mardi Gras. In the United States, only New Orleans holds a Carnival festival as Mardi Gras or Ash Tuesday.

New Orleans, Caribbean countries, and Brazil celebrate the Carnival at the same time, normally the end of February, but every fourth year it begins in the early March. It is suspected that Carnival has some relationship with Christianity because the pinnacle of Carnival, Ash Tuesday, is exactly forty days before the Easter. Even as the Roman Empire officially recognized Christianity, it continued to embrace many eastern pagan customs, including Carnival.

Carnival was even celebrated in Korea, right after the Korean War in 1955. A famous poet, Noh Chun Myung, led the celebration (射肉祭) on the banks of the Han river in Seoul. Unfortunately it was not continued when popular opinion condemned Carnival as a decadent *après-guerre* custom.

Brazil's Carnival was imported by Portuguese colonists. Brazil has a peculiar carnival tradition of throwing water on the passers-by. This practice came from the Hindu religious ceremony called Holi, which was imported by way of Portugal's colony Goa in India. The mass appeal and beauty of the Brazilian carnival is the marching of people in a variety of colorful costumes under the command of a leader along with imperial court nobles, all dancing and singing to Samba music.

The Brazilian Carnival was developed and encouraged by white farmers, who saw it as a way of releasing stress for the slaves who work arduously under tropical climate. With the introduction of Carnival, the working efficiency rose drastically. Brazil government gave incentives to promote the festival so that it became one of the sources of foreign hard currency to Brazilian economy.

All Brazilian obstetric hospitals are alarmed to prepare for "Carnival babies" 280 days after Carnival season. There is competition among samba schools during the Carnival parade. The winner gets plenty of prizes. A lot of worldwide tourists come to Brazil every year to see the Brazilian Carnival.

During Carnival season, many accidents occur due to too many people gathering, singing, dancing, and drinking, but it is relatively safe because of enhanced police surveillance during this festival.

I believe Brazilians are very smart to celebrate this kind of big festival organized by the government to release people's stress on a yearly basis.

yeonbw@hotmail.com

STORIES

Wanted God
Soo Sup Byun

1

Afterward, I couldn't figure out why I tried to kill myself. I might have done it as a joke out of boredom to kill time. It seemed so because others said so, but when I thought it over, it wasn't like that. I shouldn't feel any urge for suicide since at that time I fell into deep thought about something. Or perhaps it happened because I was unable to get out of the maze of thoughts.

After a big disturbance, I was expelled to another place. In other words, I was moved from Paradise Garden to God's City. I merely knew that because the newcomers to the Garden said so. I didn't know where I was going because the magnetic floating train passed the tunnel so fast. I just felt I was on the same route as when I went to Paradise Garden.

I was in a good mood when I went to the Garden, but now I was afraid. Besides, there was nobody else in the train, so I felt somewhat lonely. If anybody was there, I could talk and ask what would happen to me, but I couldn't. I was worrying whether I would be able to work as before. It was a vague idea that I seemed to have been doing some kind of work, though I couldn't remember what. Or maybe it was a long time ago.

Getting off the train, I saw a guide board at the ticket gate. As I passed by, a voice rang out, "Stop and get the instruction guide!" As I stopped in front of the board, my features appeared on the screen, and the voice continued.

"Welcome to your move-in, Dr. Ha! What kind of work would you like to do here?"

I wasn't sure what to do. "Well! Do I have to work?"

The answer was a sound of disgust.

"Everybody from Paradise Garden seems to be the same! Here you have to solve everything by yourself. To do that, you have to work. Let me see. Last time, you made robots here. But you won't be able to find that kind of job anymore, although some positions are still available in the field of spirit or human ecology."

In deep thought, I stared at the screen. All of a sudden, I felt fear. I worried about what I could really do.

"Can I choose the job a little later, after I look around a little bit?"

"Look around? This is not Paradise Garden. Whoever came like you never returned here."

"They might have found jobs directly."

"If so, that would be nice! But all of them were found dead on the streets. Most of them were killed or starved to death. Anyway, do whatever you would like to do. It's your choice."

Thinking about death, I felt something strange. I didn't know when I first had this vague idea.

"Isn't there any other employment agency?"

"There is one on the road toward the city and another one on the road going out of the city. But you cannot come and go freely. It will be decided on the basis of your merits and demerits. In your case, only returning here can secure your safe residence."

"It's very interesting. Since when has this system been in effect?"

A doubtful voice came out.

"You really don't know? The system was made by Nool Ha. Isn't Dr. Ha's first name Nool?"

Surprised, I laughed.

"Before the new era in human history, I had heard of the restrictions of residence by the communists, but indeed history repeats itself. A dictator named the same as me must have done it."

"Well! I don't know about that. I don't care what that was. This system works best in our time. So, what are you going to do?"

Hesitating, I asked, "What kind of jobs did you say are available? Oh, it's on the screen. Manifestation of spirit and research on human ecology! Well, the manifestation of spirit sounds like an absurd one in this era of science, but the research on human ecology sounds interesting."

"Then we will indicate that you will work in the research laboratory on human ecology. Please go out through Exit 11. By the grace of God, I hope you will achieve good results so that you can go back to Paradise Garden again."

2

I came out through an exit. I thought it was only an illusion of my eyesight, but immediately I realized it wasn't Exit 11 but Exit 1. As I tried to return, a voice came out like thunder.

"Without wasting energy, let Mr. Nool Ha in! I have something to talk to him about."

After some kind of plasma phenomenon, a man appeared in brilliant light. I thought it might be a hologram, not a man. But I wasn't sure of it. For no reason, I felt that I had to kneel down. My eyes were so dazzled that I couldn't see him, even though I tried very hard.

"Who on earth are you? How do you know my name?"

A mysterious echoing sound spread.

"I am the one who exists by myself!"

I responded bluntly, as if he were talking nonsense. "I know there is nobody who exists by himself. From the way you are talking about the things which were discussed by religious people before the new era, I suppose you must be an old man in your second childhood, like me, who can neither die or live."

He burst out laughing. As he stopped, I felt a strong energy discharge and a chill over my body.

"Look at me! You will know who I am."

I looked up at him. With a big bang, a character appeared in hologram. I felt again the same illusionary symptom in my eyesight as when I mistook Exit 1 for Exit 11 before. It carried some of my own features some time ago. I could not understand it at all. Perhaps I might have seen the god who resembled me because he was created by me, although I did not think so. The god might have resembled me before the new era, but it seemed absurd to believe it so in this almighty machine era! Seeing myself talking to myself, I thought I might be going insane. I started to laugh like a crazy man and murmured, "Please don't test me anymore. Don't make me confused. Even though recently there are some who call themselves god, I am not that crazy. Please wipe out my cubic picture and show me your original features. I only tried to kill myself and was kicked out of the Garden."

Again I heard the voice like thunder. "You defiled me. And you are depreciating yourself! I forgive you because you are stupid enough to kill yourself. Otherwise I would resolve this right away."

I laughed again.

"Anyway, who are you? Who on earth are you, making me laugh? I am sick and tired of living too. I'd prefer not to exist!"

I felt like falling into a strong magnetic field, a black hole, and all the parts of my body were dissolved. And the echoing sound was gradually repeating and getting louder.

"You defiled me. You defiled me. You …"

Amazed, I burst into laughter again.

"I didn't defile anybody."

Again the thunderous echoing voice spread.

"You defiled your god who took care of you until now! I am the god who has had patience with your defilement and loves you! And yet, you insist you don't know me?"

I could not help but burst into uncontrollable laughter.

"You made me laugh. Where is this god? Why do we, who were repeatedly duplicated, need god? Human beings live once and die, with a limited life, so they create a god themselves for eternal life. But man-made creatures like us can prolong our lives now by changing parts of machinery even if we cannot duplicate ourselves, so why do we need a god?"

The so-called god got so angry that it made me tremble with fear.

"I've never forgiven anyone who denied me. But because I love you, I forgive you. I am the god of your love. You must believe that."

I laughed again.

"I'd rather disappear forever than live in the world like this as a so-called god, but since I cannot do that either, why should I have any pity?"

The so-called god soothed me with a soft voice.

"You should know suicide is a crime. Since you denied god, it meant you were not in awe of life. Because you committed such crime, you were expelled from Paradise Garden! Anyhow, you have to know who you are before anything else."

3

"Who am I? Well, who am I? He called me Nool Ha, but I don't know why I have to exist! He said I made Nool Ha's law to limit residence, but I don't know what he was talking about. The so-called god said he loves me, but why does he love only me? He should love everybody! Seeing such a being calling himself a god, all the gods might disappear! Well, I am a machine whose parts have been changed a few times, surely, then who am I?"

I recalled that after coming out of Exit 1, the magnetic floating train I took passed a long tunnel like a wormhole. As the train came above ground, it stopped in front of a cave surrounded by a huge forest. Somebody announced it was the final stop. When I got off, a small car was already waiting there. I got into the car through some strange power. Unlike the train, the car ran so slowly that I felt almost bored. A screen like an aurora blocked the front, and a three-dimensional image appeared. The screen moved with the car in a certain distance, showing the words "Welcome to Cave City from Paradise Garden" and "God saved human beings and established a self-governing district here." Suddenly, a nuclear bomb exploded, and the mushroom cloud went up and spread. With a conditioned reflex, I bent down my head. Then the automatic voice system installed in the car said, "It's only an image, so don't worry."

On the three-dimensional screen, the Third World War was starting. Before the new era, as fossil fuel ran out in America and China, the local warfare from the disputes among countries for the interest in oil spread broadly over the South China Sea area and developed into a World War, a collision between Western and Oriental culture.

A fierce fire, caused by the use of nuclear bombs to compete for power, wiped out almost all the human beings on Earth. Most human beings died, and whoever was left alive had to endure the long winter brought by the nuclear clouds that blocked the sun permanently and suffered from diseases caused by the radiation. In addition, the explosive power of nuclear bombs altered the axis of Earth. The latitude tilted about thirty degrees, and as a result, the tropical zone became a temperate zone and the temperate zone became a frigid zone.

In Cave City, an underground bunker that was prepared for nuclear war in Washington, DC, enabled some of its residents to escape death at the time. On the screen showed the names of scientists who made contributions to saving human beings. To my surprise, my name, Nool Ha, appeared next to Neul Ha. While Nool Ha was named as chairman of the World Scientist Association, Neul Ha didn't have any official title. Although I tried hard to recall him, such a scientist's name wasn't in my memory. But I seemed to know the next name on the list, a molecular biologist, Hella Ha. And Na Ha, Yi Ha, and Sam Ha might be relatives of mine, since we have the same family name. The names following them looked unfamiliar. Roughly counted, it happened a half century before the new era. *If I am Nool Ha, how old am I?* Besides, I didn't know the relation between that era and the new era. I was anxious to know why and when the new era started.

Hella appeared on the screen. She looked familiar. Since I had been doing nothing but filling up my energy at Paradise Garden, my brain might have degenerated too, or my memory might have been erased by mistake when new information was put into my brain. Anyway, I felt something was wrong. Perhaps I might be hallucinating, just like my illusionary sight.

The three-dimensional image of Hella came closer to my heart. "Since we are going to create humans as autotrophs, stop killing each other for existence." She said that the experiment to graft photosynthetic autotrophs on humans was completed.

The moving vegetable man vaguely reminded me of some terrible accident. At that time, everybody under the ground bunker trembled from the fear of being killed. Because of bitter cold and radiation from nuclear bombs outside of the underground bunker, we couldn't go out and we couldn't get any food. Due to the shortage of stored food, everybody was suffering from starvation. Thus, people started to kill each other openly by the law of jungle. Under such circumstances, the only way to survive was becoming a human-made photosynthetic autotroph, or a robot.

See, all my body parts are made of machine parts; I assumed that I might have become a robot. I don't even know if my own brain is a human brain or an accumulated circuit of electrons. Gradually I revive a vague memory of me wandering around in the bombed area. In the radiation, my whole body and soul couldn't survive as a living thing. It is obvious that I am not a human being. However, I don't understand why the so-called god treated me as a human being. It might be because he wanted me to stay in Garden to embody the spirit of human being.

Hella is the true nature whom I've dreamed of for a long time, isn't she?

Although it was a short period of time, she seemed to be my companion. Indeed, a robot has a partner, so I might have one too. When I thought so, it seemed to be so. From the continuous chain of memories returning to me, it seems that I might be a human. Or at least one part of my body might still have the electrochemical function supported not by photosynthetic battery but by ATP (Adenosine triphosphate).

The yearning for Hella was revived again. It obviously indicates I am a human. I still feel the sorrow of separating from her at the time. I had to pass through the bombed area contaminated with radiation to go to another underground bunker. That's how I parted from her.

If Hella is also a robot like me, whose body parts were replaced by machine parts several times, I thought that she might be still in this Cave City. But if she became a vegetable human, how long would she have lived even if she survived?

It came to my mind that I had to look for Hella. I felt she might be around somewhere. Later I figured out that the endless desire of humans made the residents who couldn't find satisfaction decide to get out of the bunker, exposing themselves to the sun and radiation and becoming like trees. To stop human desire, the restriction of residence was advised under the name of the Chairman of the Scientist Association. And it looked like Hella used my name. Yet I don't understand why the law of Nool Ha still exists. For a few centuries, the underground bunker was changed to underground cave. Due to the heredity of ancestors, they could not go to the outside world, because they could become autotrophs through man-made rays or unmovable trees by direct sun. In other words, the outside forest would be considered to be humans who gave up to be tree men. But at night, they could come out of the cave, like bats, and move around. The shock of the nuclear explosion moved Earth's latitude thirty degrees to the north, so they were at sixty-five degrees north latitude. Hence, summer was short and winter was long. However, they didn't have too much time to enjoy the night, either, because of the cold.

In desire for more pleasure, some of them stayed longer and met the morning sun. Consequently, their feet spread into the soil like roots to search for water. They could not move, so they screamed and died. The scream from one of these accidents echoed into the cave, and it made the residents tremble. This didn't occur often. Thus, the next night, people held a religious festival for the dead and engraved his name on the stump, like a chiseled tombstone, so that people alive could remember. They prayed for his other life by applying on their foreheads the stroma sap that came down instead of blood wherever the chisel cut. The movie ended with the image of a screaming human being. The night view in the cave was bright.

When I got out of the car, someone was waiting. He looked like a black man with a green face. His eyes were so bright that he reminded me of a wild cat in the darkness. I wasn't surprised because I saw the features of human being already in the three-dimensional image. They had been changed so much that even the true features of a human being were hard to see. Since the DNA itself was changed, I didn't know how my face was changed. I thought it was me because they said so.

"Welcome, Mr. Nool Ha! We are much honored with your visit to our Cave City. Allow me to greet you as mayor, representing all the citizens."

I sighed. After human beings were under control of environments in this way for a few centuries, it might have been inevitable for human races to be altered from the time when human history began. I put out my hand. He held my hand and whispered, "Mr. Nool Ha! You'd better stay quiet and leave. It's god's order."

Surprised, my face quivered convulsively.

"Thanks a lot. How do you remember my name, which even I forgot? You keep saying god, god, but what kind of god is he? I met him, too, but when did he appear in the present world so that we could see him? And yet I don't understand why he has obstructed my free will and keeps harassing me."

He seemed to be hard to deal with.

"God would watch us. If something goes wrong, I am afraid of his retaliation."

I felt uneasy at his fearful look.

"While god is said to be love, if he invokes fear, he must not be a god. The conqueror must act as a god. Who on earth is he, watching me all the time and harassing me? Well, there are no mural paintings in the ceiling of the cave—only a moving camera! Tens of thousands of years ago, life in the cave was free, but how pitiful is the god who watches everyone all the time. Why the hell are you afraid of him so much? If he's a real god, he shouldn't be a conqueror who killed human beings; instead, he should be love itself. His moving eyes should be focused on those who refuse to be human and become trees."

"I'd like to hear that."

"Indeed! About the contents on the screen, who made the movie? And what did Mr. Nool Ha do?"

"Let's celebrate for our god. Now! Let's go over there and worship our god. I will show you how much our god loves us."

Instead of answering my question, he said this extravagant thing and took me to the noisy crowd.

"Pardon me, Mr. Nool Ha. I acted like this because I didn't want to incur god's anger. God satisfies us in everything. As long as we don't disobey him, we can lead a comfortable life. As I said, he is the god of love, but he also punishes fearfully."

"How does he punish? When did he appear here?"

He started to talk about their history. About a half century before the new era, the World War erupted and within three months the earth was ruined by nuclear bombs. Some people were saved by Dr. Hella and became green humans, but they had to live underground. Meanwhile, the robots, which were unaffected by radiation, somehow were taught the consciousness of human beings and tried to conquer the humans.

"The robots actually took over the whole human world. The invading robots took away all rights from humans and made them follow their orders. Humans were too weak to fight and were killed by the spiritless robots on a large scale, like flies wiped out by insecticide. Humans' weapons were merely guns for self-defense, knives for home use, or stones as used in the Stone Age, while the robots were armed with laser beams for killing and strong magnetic-field devices, and so humans couldn't even get close to the robots. The robots had brains equipped with highly specialized military tactics, and their eyes could exert control at near and far distances and detect organic substances by ultra-red rays. All their soldiers possessed telepathic ability, so resistance meant death. Thus, they were called 'god's army.'"

He sighed. All of a sudden I remembered something. It was a robot model of future soldiers who would be put in an imaginary war, but they were controlled from far away. I couldn't figure out how they went to war with self-consciousness.

"Who was the commander of the army?"

He stopped thinking, searched my expression, and talked cautiously.

"Well! As I mention god's troops, I suddenly realize, after considering the situation that occurred next, that it was you who came for the invasion, didn't you? Well! I didn't experience it, but I heard of it. And the conqueror's name was recorded in history, which clearly resembled your name, so you at the present time and at that time might be the same person, correct? Or it might be a different person with the same name. Indeed, there are so many duplicated people—"

Surprised so much, I almost fainted.

"Did you say he was using my name and resembled me? Thus the law of Nool Ha was made at the time?"

"It didn't seem so! Before, it wasn't a law but an acknowledged matter to protect us green people, but they seemed to adopt it as a law to prevent humans from uniting. It was because there were clearly differences in time."

"Could you tell me about the war situation in detail?"

He laughed loudly. "As I told you before, it could not be called a war. They had to surrender unconditionally after a few people were burnt by laser beam or electrocuted by an electric-field in the battle. Besides, since they were green people, they became obedient like grass-eating animals or trees, and even if there were a few who resisted, they got killed immediately."

"Well, how have they been ruled since that time?"

"We are under the god's rule! We just obey god's words."

I repeated him. "God's rule! How does god rule?"

As if not understanding, he stared at me.

"Are you testing me? You don't look like you came from another star or woke up in a hibernation casket a couple of days ago! And yet you don't look like a human duplicated by mistake. Since you came here in the magnetic floating train, you must have come here by god's order. But you say you don't know god's rule. I really don't understand."

He might be right, because I met the god just a little while ago and came to this cave by his order. I couldn't see his features, but I saw his powerful effect. Obviously it was the same as the appearance of a god tens of centuries ago. Concerning the question of whether god came from another star, human beings can merely rotate within the solar system but cannot set foot beyond. Robots could go out tens of light-years to look for a reliable place to live by utilizing universal waves as energy and changing their parts whenever needed, but indeed a human like me can neither be classified as a human nor a machine. And I was interested in the hibernation casket and duplicated humans. I felt vaguely that I might have gone through the process.

"What if someone was against god's rule?"

"They took him out and made him a tree to make him silent."

As a machine decomposed, god ordered somebody not to deprive energy from me when I entered Exit 1 by illusion. If my energy were deprived, I might become a nonliving thing, yes? Why did god say I had to know myself, who is nobody in particular? God knows well that the green human becomes a tree whose roots spread into the ground for more water after the foliage gets activated by sunlight, and thick leaves broaden its surface area for more carbonic acid gas. It doesn't sound like the so-called god's providence; they certainly used indirectly the articles acknowledged by Nool Ha. Suddenly I thought of Hella. I felt an irresistible yearning for her all over my body. In this way, I seem to be a human being, but when I touch my body, I feel it is just a carbon structure, a synthetic inorganic substance, not an organic living body, through which electric energy is flowing instead of the chemical energy obtained from blood circulation.

"Indeed god is omnipotent. Your honorable mayor, do you know about Dr. Hella, who was converted into an autotroph for the existence of human beings? Seeing her hologram on the screen when I came to the cave, I feel she's still alive."

He looked solemn, and his face changed to a darker green. After clearing his throat once, he spoke decisively.

"Of course I know her. Dr. Hella is a living myth to us. So is Dr. Nool Ha. But I am still in a deep doubt whether you are the original one or a duplicated one. Mr. Nool Ha, you just look like the doctor both in the picture and the three-dimensional projection! However, when I hear you talk, you don't sound like him."

Even I myself couldn't decide if it's me or somebody else. Indeed, as god said, I may have to find out who I really am first.

"Let me see. I don't even know if I am an original human or a duplicated human, How long ago on Earth did Dr. Nool Ha work?"

Watching my movements again, he made irrelevant remarks. He seemed to wondering if I were a spy of god. "We don't have any reason at all to disobey god in our green human city. We make our living in accordance with the scripture of god. We always pray to god. We also thank Hella when we take auto-nutrition. Really! On the death-day of Dr. Hella, we hold a celebratory festival, even though we cannot call it a death-day!"

"Isn't it a death-day? What do you mean?"

Thinking of something, he spoke privately. "Because of Dr. Hella, we have a dream. There is transmigration of spirit that only humans can enjoy. Dr. Hella suggested such a dream to us, and besides, she showed us the dream herself."

Amazed, I looked at him.

"How?"

Watching my expression, he hesitated. I explained in detail that I was sent here after being kicked out of the human garden for attempted suicide, which was a crime of disobedience to god's providence. "As more man-made humans who commonly possess human consciousness are produced, a suicide, which is usually accompanied by another suicide, becomes a crime of murder. Thus, god said to look around at the human world and try to find out yourself first. From the cold way the god treated me, you should be able to figure that you don't have to keep guard on me. It is also because, though I am composed of machine parts, I seem to be more a human being!"

Still, he spoke cautiously. "Well! We had previous instances of being executed by laser beam from the counter operation of god's spies. That's why our hope for eternal life would disappear! Although those who possess their consciousness commonly with man-made humans were sent to the hibernation casket."

"Is that so? I am anxious to know what other contributions Dr. Hella made!"

As if he was certain, he talked firmly. "I watched my mouth because I worried that Dr. Hella could be illuminated as a god. In the second Commandment of his scripture, god prohibited us from believing in any other god. When death approaches, we green people are paralyzed and then hardened like trees. Dr. Hella wanted us to become trees—which was the project for transmigration—rather than the project for resurrection, which enabled us to prolong our lives through duplication or mutual possession of consciousness. It was because a tree could live for a few thousand years. She said the spirit of a tree would be transformed to be born as human again. That's why she went out to the wilderness and met the dawn. In other words, in the brilliant sunlight, she became a tree herself. We could see the spectacle on CCTV installed outside, and so we recorded it and kept it safe. Therefore, in respecting her mind, we want to be trees. Consequently, the outdoors is full of trees."

"Ah! Really! Then which anniversary of Dr. Hella's death-day is this year?"

"Its two-hundred-first year! The two hundredth anniversary festival last year was remarkable."

I wanted to know how long ago she had lived, since I might be able to know myself better.

"Well, how long had she lived before her death?"

"She became a tree before reaching one hundred years. If she picked out the resurrection project instead of becoming a tree, she might have been living until now. She was a great person. There are groundless rumors that instead of becoming a stone, she became a tree waiting for her man. And it is said that Mr. Nool Ha is still alive, and aren't you possibly that Mr. Nool Ha? Still, I am not certain whether you are a duplicate of Mr. Nool Ha or a man-made human with the same consciousness!"

If I am the one called Nool Ha, I must have been living more than three centuries. "Well, I don't know myself either! Anyway I'd like to go to see Hella. Could you go with me?"

He thought about it seriously. "I have to think it over. If there are too many visitors for Hella, god would surely burn down the tree. Moreover, how can I give the location to the person whom god sent? I have to think it over. I don't know the exact location, just roughly whereabouts. Only the one who knows Hella well can communicate spiritually with her. If you are really Mr. Nool Ha, she would shout. I can take you near there, and that's as far as I can go."

"Then how did you do it at the last celebrating festival? It wasn't held in front of Hella?"

"You are right! We did it in front of a big tree, which we felt was right. In the end the tree was withered by god's soldiers. We believe that Hella is still alive. If you are Mr. Nool Ha, you would certainly find her. But you have to do it secretly."

Hearing his story, I felt I found some clue for something that was explained unsatisfactorily. Why did god say, "Know yourself"? A terrible suspicion suddenly occurred to me that the god might try to use me to find Hella. If he is god, he must know the answer! I felt something dumb, different from before. As I thought of her more and more, I'd like to see her, even though she is a tree. But still, I couldn't get rid of a certain feeling of uneasiness.

"Then I don't need to look for her. It's better for her to give us a dream. Perhaps they might make me look for her. If they know I can find her, even one chance in a million, and get rid of her, we'd lose even that dream. The difference between us humans and them is that humans can have a dream."

4

And yet the only place free from the nuclear danger, even for a short while, was the base at the South Pole. A group of scientists who were studying living organisms there had time to prepare for the aftermath of the nuclear explosion. Sixty degrees south at that time changed to thirty degrees south, a temperate zone. In the northern latitude, almost everything was exterminated from nuclear winter. However, in the South Pole area, less damage was done from the explosion. Therefore, nuclear aircraft carriers and nuclear submarines, as well as ships and airplanes, gathered in the southern latitude area and made a living space for human beings. But the southern latitude area could not be made safe for a while because of the enormous aftermath. The smoke from everything burning on the ground in the nuclear fire in the northern latitude, the dust clouds from storms and the radiation from the nuclear disruption started to fall down toward the south, into the atmospheric zone. Thus the nuclear winter approached the southern latitude too. When they prepared for these disasters, they heard news that the green Cave City was taken over by the man-made humans, so those scientists started to develop an underwater city. That was because they had learned that the robots were not able to be active in water.

    I am going to the underwater city, which was the last one to have wanted to be human, through a tube like wormhole in a magnetic floating train. The city is formed with water above. It wasn't that simple, seeing the conqueror who called himself god. When the thirty-year war against humans ended, they started the first year of the new era to celebrate that day, and since then, human era has disappeared from history.

When I count by Hella's death day, since I was seventy-five years old at the time of the Third World War, forty years before the new era and 201 years after the new era, I am a total of 316 years of age. It is an age which was possible to reach in the mythological era, or hero era, but impossible to reach for human beings. However, I still exist now, don't I? How could I live that long? Perhaps I might be not a human. Since my body is composed of machine parts, I might be able to survive this long, right? Or I might have spent all that time in a hibernation casket. How have I been living so long? Who am I, who wasn't my own choice, but seem to be fabricated by somebody else? I do want to know exactly how I became like this.

The above-ground city and underwater city of human beings were developed at a similar level with God's City. Here, god's administrator was governing directly. In other words, humans are ruled by robots with consciousness. Humans were beaten by machines because they fell behind in memory storage of the brain and the number of mediums for nerve transmission. While the human brain consists of about one hundred billion nerve cells and one hundred trillion synapses, machine humans can store the information at any time they want with double that number of functions. And while organic chemical energy functions within a certain limit, machine-humans can function tens times greater or more, depending on design. And although humans depend on the chemical electricity of food, a man-made human gets energy even from universal waves. Furthermore, although humans who are ruled by the environment get sick, the parts of human machines can be replaced whenever they are obsolete, worn out, or oxidized. How could humans fight against such capability?

Why did man-made humans with near omnipotence conquer the last base of the humans? It might be because even if they possessed consciousness, stored vast knowledge, and utilized the knowledge, it was merely an application. The consciousness could be transferred to them, but unconsciousness could not. Besides, they couldn't get creative ability from inspiration. The troops posed as god had to fight the war for thirty years because they recognized these problems.

Unlike Cave City, god governs this aboveground city directly, not through a trust government. This is because humans still tried to maintain their dignity, and the human machines needed the intelligence of human beings who wanted to exist. Thus, excellent scholars and artists were called to Paradise Garden. It might be a highly calculated policy to paralyze the human mind by sensual pleasure. Actually, I was treated in that way too.

It is obvious that the so-called god's group is afraid of humans because they know how hard the thirty-year war was. Therefore, even if a human machine acts like god, these people, unlike the Green Cave citizens, don't seem to believe in god. God could conquer humans with weapons, but he couldn't rule over their minds. Humans suffered from the restriction of activities by the radiation from thirty years of wartime. Especially since they couldn't get the necessities of life from the ground ruined from the explosions, they had to survive only on fish, shellfish, or seaweed. The war commodities and equipment were only leftovers from the Third World War at the most, and the fighters on the carriers couldn't fly due to lack of oil. Since the robots were not affected by the nuclear contamination, they could take the military goods and equipment leftover from the war and use those goods and equipment to kill humans. The aircraft carriers and battleships were totally destroyed by robot's attacks at the beginning of the war. Thus humans without proper weapons had to engage in the war primitively. They used guerilla warfare, such as electrocuting electric machinery with water canon, catching them with strong magnets to decompose, melting them with *aqua regia*, coating them with highly adhesive bubbles so that they could not move, or luring them out to the battleships. But the robots also altered their war strategy not to kill but capture humans if possible. They needed more brain consciousness, and thought that humans would surrender from the shortage of food in a long-term war. Also they knew humans couldn't resist anymore, given the limited human life span.

As god's patience reached its limit, the robots started to attack the humans' submarines with torpedoes. But a few submarines kept away from the attack. As a final notification, god, who got mad at the failure, warned that his army would exterminate all marine life by flowing oil over the surface of water, while they changed Earth's crust by dropping nuclear bombs in the area surrounding the ocean. As god's warning bombs made wall after wall of water, humans realized they could no longer resist the war. They floated on the water and surrendered. Their rough descendants became more resistant as they were ruled by god's iron fist. Consequently, terrors occurred more often, and man-made humans got killed. When I arrived at the city, guards sent by the administrator guided me. All the guards looked like me. They seemed to be robots or duplicated humans, so I couldn't tell who was guarding who. I felt confused; I couldn't figure out why they guarded me this much.

"I don't understand why the administrator treats me like this. I don't have any information on this city, and I was permitted only to visit this city!"

They didn't say anything. Because of the action at Cave City, I thought I might be detained. I felt more convinced about it after seeing through my back window an escort car following behind.

Finally, an accident occurred. A remote-controlled bomb blew up, and my car rocked and leaned to one side. The car behind tumbled too. The guards broke the car door, came out of the car, and searched for the enemy with laser beams. In the air, iron powder fell down like snow, and highly adhesive bubble shells flew down over and covered everything. I was covered with adhesive materials so that I couldn't move at all.

5

I woke up from the noise. A bright light shined on me. I tried to move but couldn't. I was tied to a torture board. They ridiculed me.

"Even god cannot do anything!"

I didn't understand what they meant. It sounded like they were cursing god.

They searched every corner of my body with a gamma projector.

"This guy is also a robot. Why did we guard this worthless robot?"

"You are right! Why did we do it? But he was a VIP, obviously."

"Oh, no! How did this robot get a human brain? Only the right brain. The left brain is man-made. Human brains get changed because of dementia—otherwise they might fail to function."

As he looked at the screen, the leader of them stated, "He's an interesting fellow. Check him thoroughly."

I was startled by their words. Who took away half of my brain? Why, where, when, and for whom did they take it away? They started to examine my body thoroughly again. They started to take a picture of my retina.

"There is something strange in his eyes. There are double chips in the back of his retina, and one of them looks like a transmitter! Only one eye! Someone is looking at us through this eye. Come and look at this!"

The leader stopped looking at the chip in my retina on the screen and covered my left eye with his hand. I felt the body heat of a human from his hand. They must be the human terrorists who are resisting against god, as I had heard.

"You are right. We have to pull it out. We'd better hurry to move to another agitation point. Everybody hurry up! Don't we have a cutting machine? We'd better pull out his eye. Move faster!"

With one eye pulled out, I couldn't tell distance, but I could still see them.

The absent eye confused the guards watching in front of the television screen on the street, to which the hologram was being sent. I couldn't figure out why such machinery was installed in my eye. Hurriedly they moved to another agitation point.

"This guy must be a spy. Otherwise he may be associated with god!"

I strongly denied it. "Who on earth are you? I don't know why I have to be treated like this. What is your purpose? Who ignores the dignity of human beings?"

They laughed. "Did you say the dignity of humans? Why do you inquire into the dignity of humans who are not human beings? Really, one cannot be called a human with only half of a brain!"

"Certainly I *was* a human! I don't know why I became so miserable like this!"

They laughed at me loudly again. The leader gave them an order.

"We have to make his identity clear. Maybe he's telling the truth. He could have forgotten because of dementia!

By scanning his brain and giving a shock to his nervous system, his memory might be revived."

I was tied to an iron bed again, and the holographic images appeared on the screen projected by laser beam. As the images moved, electric shock was given to various parts of my body. And every time, my whole body fell into convulsions.

"What is your name?"

"They called me Nool Ha, and so my name seems to be Nool Ha!"

They looked at each other and seemed doubtful about my answer. The leader asked, "You might have the same name, but Mr. Nool Ha lived a few centuries ago, didn't he? You must have worshiped his heroic acts for human beings, so now you even use his name!"

"Since I have been duplicated a few times, I don't know if I am an original or a duplicated human. But it is true that I was called Nool Ha!"

"How do you prove it?"

"When I came to God's City, which god governs himself, from Paradise Garden, they called me by the name. They also said the law of Mr. Nool Ha was made by me."

"Do you know what kind of law it is?"

"I don't know well, but it seems to be an absurd law prohibiting change of residence without permission!"

"Perhaps you, a duplicated human of Mr. Nool Ha, might have made it?"

"Even a duplicate of Nool Ha wouldn't make such a law to restrain human beings. Now I remember! At Cave

City, they said Nool Ha advised the green people not to go out of the cave. And somebody might have used that to make the bad law!"

"Think who that might be. Are you a first-generation duplicate? Second-generation? Third-generation? Or are you a man-made human? Think carefully! Your face looks same as theirs. Really, we couldn't distinguish the robots who guarded you. Anyway, one of them must've made the law."

"Well, it seems to be neither Na Ha, who was the first-generation duplicated human, nor Neul Ha, man-made human, who charged my consciousness with electricity, because they joined me to rescue human beings. Once I rode with a few traveling robots in a cosmic vessel that traveled between stars. But since I was in a hibernation casket, I didn't know the situation. Later on, I found out that god's army conquered the humans, and somebody impersonated me in the meantime. Who could it be? It could be the so-called god himself, couldn't it?"

As I thought deeply for the answer, they gave me an even stronger electric shock. The shock clearly distinguished the function of the right brain from the left brain. The left brain, which is a minute circuit, couldn't cope with the amount of electric discharge. It discharged the electricity to the circuit breaker at the end of my foot and twisted my whole body. The cord which tied me broke off. As the electricity was shut down, my whole body hung limp. Meanwhile, in the right brain, my retina went blank from the shock. A fantasy world appeared, and I didn't know if it was a dream or a memory. I started to hum merrily. As they realized that I was dreaming, they started to record the vision. Looking at the screen, they shouted with joy.

"We may be able to find the so-called god!"

6

"My dear Pinocchio, Neul Ha. I will even give you consciousness! Then you would be the same as a human being."

Seeing the psychoholography of my brain, I transferred my consciousness to Neul Ha by giving an electric shock to each part of his brain. At the beginning, the experiment wasn't very effective, and Neul Ha showed only mechanical attributes. He only took care of the information but wouldn't try to think. However, as theexperiment was repeated—I didn't know when—he showed some sign of creative ability.

This experiment was much harder than connecting the memory chip with the cerebrum of my duplicated human. I stored the same amount of memory as the first-generation duplicate, Na Ha; second-generation duplicate, Yi Ha; and third-generation duplicate, Sam Ha, and compared their ability with Neul Ha. It was a great outcome that we could store unlimited amounts of information in all of them. But the duplicated human made me realize the limited ability of the human being. They took out only a little bit from so much knowledge and hoarded most information. However, Neul Ha could take out any information that was put in at any time. He could assemble a lot more robots than duplicated humans, almost without any mistakes. But depending on their mood, humans and duplicated humans ruined the works. So Neul Ha was enough for me to love.

At the time, dark clouds covered the international situation, and people were haunted with fear. Thus, the most popular program was about the second advent of god. The prophecy that there would be god's judgment on June 6 at six o'clock was the best seller. The software program about how to survive was sold in the black market. Na Ha said Sam Ha set up a program to his cerebral chip to survive. Yi Ha was waiting for a better program.

As the Third World War became a nuclear war, I tried to save the humans by leading a robot division with Na Ha and Neul Ha. When I recalled the holography in my brain, all the living things looked like trash burning in a dump. The Geiger counter kept ringing according to the density of contaminated radiation. Even the radiation inhaler was useless because it emitted backward from being overloaded. The lead clothes for cutting off radiation were useless too. Na Ha and I almost became exposed to too much radiation. Neul Ha and the robot division were not restrained by such things, but they showed abnormal phenomena from excessive bombing.

We planned to travel between stars for four and half centuries until the nuclear contamination disappeared on Earth. While the robots would travel by using the cosmic wave for energy, I, a human, and Na Ha would dream and envision in the hibernation caskets. Yi Ha and Sam Ha refused to go with us, asserting that they would live by divine providence.

When we returned from the trip between stars, Earth had entered the era of duplicated and man-made humans. During the thirty years that I was in the hibernation casket, all the human beings were conquered. It was evident that in the meantime I went to some other world. Since I was dreaming and envisioning, it might possibly be a world of fantasy or spirit, which was said to exist in human beings. However, it was an entirely different world from Proxima of Centaurus, which was four light years away and was mentioned by Neul Ha. Neul Ha wouldn't lie because he was a machine. Thus, I obviously dreamed of a different world. Besides, I felt it was a different dimensional world.

"Neul Ha! Certainly I went to another world and came back. Didn't you feel my consciousness? Actually, I might have dreamed it in the hibernation casket. Why didn't you wake me up instead of leaving me alone for so long?"

Neul Ha looked sad and replied quietly. "When we woke up, Na Ha had died from a vacuum inside of the cosmic vessel. We put him back into the hibernation casket, but he became a mummy. We didn't need air and wanted to prevent oxidation and discharge. We realized humans were different from us at the time. That's why we didn't wake up Dr. Ha. What else could we do?"

I regretted deeply Na Ha's unnecessary death. The grief made me forget to ask the details of the trip between stars. I smelled some kind of conspiracy, but I jumped to the conclusion that a machine was honest and wouldn't lie. "What a pity my duplicate passed away! Oh, what a pity! God took him away. He should be in the beautiful world I saw."

"If I die, can I go to such a world too?"

"Well, you have the same consciousness as me, and didn't you see the dream that I dreamed during that time?"

"No. I've never dreamed."

"Is that so? But I gave to Neul Ha everything I've got! It means that there is unconsciousness beyond the human consciousness! In the end, we cannot transfer it! Yet I gave you everything."

Neul Ha showed great interest. "Did you say unconsciousness? It sounds like a story of four centuries ago, but now, when advanced brain science has made it possible to provide information by man-made neurons, I cannot understand at all that there is unconsciousness at the bottom of consciousness. Are you saying that illusion, vision, and dream are unconsciousness? If you say you dream, then I'd better believe it. According to the theory that was put in my brain, it was explained by the quantum field that is nonlocality, which has a special character, so we can receive information without the exchange of energy. It really sounds strange. I acknowledge the exchange of information can be done without wire, by telepathy using electromagnetic fields, and sometimes different images appear from mistakes in the circuit and give us trouble. But do you dream? If you dream, it might be the sole characteristic that only the organic human brain possesses."

It was the information on consciousness that was put in Neul Ha. When I thought, until now, that the structure of Neul Ha's brain, to which the consciousness was transferred, wasn't holographed, I felt a bit doubtful. The man-made humans seemed to be responsible for the death of Na Ha, often with friction between them. They couldn't kill me because he would lose the consciousness that we mutually possessed.

"Then we don't need to talk about either dream or spirit. I created you and gave you everything, but I couldn't do it because it was god's share that created humans. Right?"

Man-made humans sent and allowed humans to live in the Garden that they made for humans on the ruined ground, who possessed consciousness mutually with them. I owed them the right to be able to go to the Garden. Thus, I pledged myself to study whether humans have unconsciousness and an after-death world. It was because I felt confident that the world I saw in my illusionary state in the hibernation casket was not three-dimensional, but a different dimensional world. It might be god's world that only humans could have.

One day, all of a sudden, they said god came to earth and announced that the day when God's Nation was founded started the new era. By god's order, I was sent to Paradise Garden. I thought I might have fallen into the dreamy illusionary state again. But Paradise Garden was clearly different from the one that I saw in the last illusionary state. Paradise Garden on the ground was used only for sightseeing and rearing humans. God's world, which I saw in my last dreamy illusionary state, seemed to be an eternal world of dream. And it gave me some doubt about the god who was said to come again. I had almost lost my life when I tried to fall into the dream state to search for god.

Who is the person who pretends to be a god? Without doubt, he seems to be the one to me. Is he the person who tried to experience the world of unconsciousness and acted like a god after stealing half of my brain? Really, I don't know when half of my brain disappeared. I don't know because I almost lost my life many times. Neul Ha traveled with me between the stars, and so he wouldn't have time enough to conquer humans and act like a god. Obviously he wouldn't take a chance to take away my brain, since he could lose his consciousness as soon as I die. If Neul Ha detained me in the hibernation casket and went out to conquer humans, then he could be god. Well! Could a man-made human play a trick? Indeed, since I gave my consciousness and lied, it might be possible for him to do the same thing. However, noticing that I, who commonly possessed consciousness with him, didn't sense it, it might not be possible. Then, might it be the ambitious Yi Ha? Or was it Sam Ha who believed in the advent of god? Perhaps god might have come again. Otherwise, it might be some other unsuspected person.

I might have to create who is the god. And tell God's World what I have seen.

7

I went back to God's City, where god lives. I stood at the ticket gate for the magnetic floating train. In a half-transparent mirror, I saw my eye had been attached again, as good as before. I rolled over the pupil of my eye and found it was same as before. I felt as if all the past events were a dream. A voice message came out of the screen.

"Dr. Ha! Welcome on your safe return. God was looking for you for a long time. Please enter Exit 1."

"Anyway, I was going to pay my respects to the god. Thank you."

As I entered Exit 1, god's voice echoed like thunder as before. Perhaps they knew with whom they were dealing, so it sounded like an amplified machine.

"I didn't give you permission to go in and out. I have to remove your energy."

As soon as he said that, the electricity in my body was gone with a flash. As I was passing out, I shouted with all my might.

"I am Nool Ha. I am your Nool Ha!"

God got mad and replied with a thunderous voice that almost made me deaf.

"Did you say you are Nool Ha? Nool Ha came back already a little while ago. Who the hell are you? Who the hell are you without identification?"

As all the energy left my body, I began to lose consciousness. As I breathed heavily and struggled, the light similarly started to flicker. On the three-dimensional screen, a person who resembled me appeared.

"Who has your identification?"

A man arrived. He was the leader of the humans who had tortured me.

"Are you a god who doesn't even know it? I am a human who is trying to get rid of you, who pretended to be a god."

Even before I finished answering, I heard an explosion that shook the shrine. God was hit, and smoke started to come out of his body. He tried to absorb the energy with all his might. But he couldn't make the effort because his body was melted by *aqua regia*. He made great efforts to maintain god's dignity to the end.

"Those who tried to harm me would get divine punishment."

God was definitely not a duplicated human, but a man-made human who was made of metal. The human leader burst out laughing, which echoed through the whole shrine.

"Did you say divine punishment? You are the very one who has to be punished!"

Then there was another explosion. Highly adhesive bubbles covered god's body and flew down. Losing all my energy, I felt something like death.

"The so-called god was you, Neul Ha! Neul Ha, you …"

soosufb@gmail.com

Practicing to Depart
Min Jung Kim

When Mr. Kim climbed to the top of the Chungpadong hill in one breath, his heavy breathing pressed all the way up against his chin. He had to stop walking and gather his breath. In the cold air, white vapor puffed out of his mouth like smoke.

With the collar of his coat soaked in sweat, in the autumn wind he felt a chill running down his spine.

Upon entering his house, Mr. Kim opened the kitchen door that connected to the two rooms aligned side by side. Since the kitchen was tightly shut all night, the smell of briquette and another cough-provoking smell bitterly stung his nose. He placed to one side of the stove all the fresh produce he just bought from the market—bean sprouts, tofu, frozen pollock, and a few spices—and then he poured out the boiling water from the aluminum pot. The briquette still had a white glow, as if it were about to breathe its last heap of breath. Flustered, Mr. Kim replaced the briquette with a fresh one and finally let out a sigh of relief.

In this particular house on top of the hill, five families lived as tenants besides Mr. Kim and his wife. A new day began with the awakening sound of children going to school, but Mr. Kim could not call it a home of the living ever since his wife became half paralyzed. The room was just physically and passively occupied.

"Mr. Kim … I guess the briquette is not in good condition again?" To-Li's mother cracked open the kitchen door and asked.

"Actually, the briquette's fine today. I just changed it."

"Instead of doing that all the time, you should put it on top of our burner."

To-Li's family occupied two rooms, a small room and an adjacent one, which gave them some leeway in terms of space.

"I don't know if today's weather will be as nice as yesterday's, but the air is cold."

Mr. Kim, before putting rice into the rice cooker, opened the window. Apologies arose in his mind. His wife slightly turned her head then, perhaps because of the chill.

His wife's senses and mental consciousness returned to a more normal state. She was able to watch television and even support herself in a cripple's gait by using one hand, raising and lowering the upper and lower neck. There was no indication that the function of her tongue was going to return. However, Mr. Kim could detect the return of her senses from the fact that she refused to take three rice meals in one day. It became a general rule of thumb that as soon as she ate something, it was discharged as excrement. She intentionally refused to eat so that no one would have to clean up after her. This very act of denial showed hope because it was a sign of her mind working. At the same time, because she suppressed this natural instinct, life became an existence of punishment. This kind of life drove her to experience recurrent instances of annoyance and frustration.

Just last autumn, Grandmother Kim's four limbs were normal, and she was full of life. During that time, the elderly couple somehow married off their four daughters, and they decided to live comfortably, moving into the present house with its many rooms.

One of the neighbors, named Sul-Ha, who had no children and lived an independent life, tried everything to please the elderly couple. But Grandmother Kim did not try to understand Sul-Ha because of her closed heart and disheveled mind concerning many other matters. Since Grandmother Kim had a hard time going to the market, and she hated the senseless conversations exchanged among the garrulous female neighbors. Neither did she bother to understand Mr. Kim's heart. Instead she scolded him. Mr. Kim, who was used to his wife's complaints, usually listened with one ear but let it out through the other. When they were coming back from a picnic outing last year in the fall, she suddenly collapsed and became paralyzed.

Mr. Kim was speculating over the reasons why it happened and couldn't really think of anything, except for one possibility. Every time his wife went up and down Chungpadong Hill, she couldn't catch her breath and sweated profusely and unusually. At the time, Mr. Kim thought that it was simply due to lack of exercise.

When Mr. Kim saw that the smoke from the burning

briquette rose to a certain level, he walked over to the kitchen burners with a heartfelt intent to cook some gruel from yesterday's leftover rice. But To-Li's mother's screaming broke the silence inside the house once again.

"I'm sick of this! If I tell you many times to wake up, then you should get up. If you do, you wouldn't have to hear me screaming at you! Why is it that children take after their parents?"

Maybe To-Li's mother was exhausted from having to raise so many children. In any case, she went out into the yard and added hot water to the cold water she just scooped up and continued to complain to herself.

"By screaming like that, do I expect to fix their habits in one morning? Only my feelings just get hurt."

The widow, who was washing the rice next to her, twisted her lips in displeasure and rudely interrupted. "Oh my goodness, Mr. Kim, you're out already? Children have so much to learn, don't they? Are you planning to heat up some gruel?"

To-Li's mother stole a glance at the widow who lived in the adjacent room.

"Well, that would be nice, but my wife absolutely refuses to eat anything," said Mr. Kim.

To-Li's mother started conversing with Mr. Kim. "That's why you should find someone as soon as possible. A live-in nanny would be appropriate, don't you think?"

The widow expressed a look of disapproval. "Is Mr. Kim purposely not hiring anyone? Isn't it because there is no one suitable?"

Ever since that morning, something did not sit right in

the mind of To-Li's mother, and she spat on the widow's words.

Out of all the tenants, To-Li's family had lived there the longest. They lived there even before Mr. Kim moved in. To-Li's husband, Pang, who was a carpenter, heard from a friend that he could transfer housing property from state ownership to private ownership without a permit. So he bought a house, but it proved to be a bad investment move and all the money was blown away. Then they were forced, once again, to move to the tenant house in Chungpadong.

It happened when they already had a huddle of four children, so they weren't able to do much of anything or go anywhere as a family because of Pang's bad drinking habits.

Something happened on the very day when Mr. Kim and his wife first moved into Chungpadong. After the elderly couple unpacked all of their basic lifelong belongings, they got too tired to start organizing, so they went to bed in order to get an early start the next morning. Someone came into their room, shouting in a thunderous voice. Mr. Kim grabbed the intruder's throat and dragged him to the front yard to hit him, only to find that it was the carpenter Pang himself, completely drunk.

When Mr. Kim first moved in, there were tenants living there already whose rooms were aligned along a straight line. Starting from the most recent tenants, the first room was occupied by a young woman who went out to cabarets; the second room, by a widow and her daughter who barely made their living as tailors for the market; the third by two young women who worked in the factory; and the next room a chauffer and his wife who were expecting a child in the near future. In the fifth room, which was connected to another room, To-Li's family lived there. When To-Li's family first moved in, they only had two daughters, but because they wanted a son, things turned out to be the way they were.

Today Mr. Kim wanted to give his wife a bath because his youngest daughter, Mal-Ja, and her husband were coming.

Ever since his wife became paralyzed, Mr. Kim was usually the one who gave her a bath. Since he couldn't bring her to a public bathhouse, there was no other way than moving her into a big rubber bucket. Washing her was not an easy job.

His daughters, who lived close by but scattered in different parts of Seoul, took turns to visit them once in a while. They were busy housekeepers, too, so it was not easy for them to visit once a week or every ten days.

In such a situation, there was no one to depend on or to blame. Mr. Kim had to sufficiently prepare everything for his wife's bath. The housekeeper entered the front gate at exactly 9:00 a.m. She had to prepare breakfast for her children, who were attending elementary school and junior high school, so she was also not in any position to help him.

"Oh my, you already got everything ready?"

The housekeeper was bubbling over with excitement when she arrived, which meant she felt either guilty or just relieved for not having to do the work herself. Mr.

Kim already brought the bucket of water into the room and pulled out the towel and undergarments.

He poured the warm water, which the housekeeper passed on to him, into the rubber bucket and took off his wife's clothes.

Ever since his wife came home from the hospital, her body became lighter, and now she was even lighter than ten days ago when he gave her last bath. She always had good skin. Because she still weighed considerably, it was not easy to boost her in a sitting position and place her inside the large rubber bucket. But now that he learned some tricks, it was somewhat easier.

When the hot water touched his wife's body, she twisted her face into a scowl and shuddered in horror, but soon her body relaxed and looked comfortable. It was called a bath, but he could not wash her as thoroughly as he could have done in a public bathhouse. He realized this as he rubbed off a lot of dirt from her skin. The dirt had accumulated even though she stayed inside the room all day. It seemed even when human beings left their bodies alone, various excrements still come out of the body through the pores of the skin. With ten days past, the surface of the bathwater was immediately covered with floating yeast-like dirt with a sour smell.

Those people in the neighborhood who didn't have much to do with their time often gossiped about the grandmother's good fortune and her devoted husband, not realizing the hardship Mr. Kim was going through.

His wife just turned sixty this year, but her skin was snowy white and smooth like a baby's skin. Whenever Mr.

Kim washed his wife, he was surprised that having lived with her in the same room for forty years, he still didn't know the details of her body. Her hips were like the shape of a drum, and her breasts were as round and taut as those of a young woman.

When he finished giving her the bath, the housekeeper put her clothes on and laid her down. Mr. Kim refreshed himself in the outdoor breeze and breathed a sigh. Today, more than any other days, the wild chrysanthemums that mutely blossomed under the rays of the autumn sun were saddening his heart.

Grandmother Kim was about to fall asleep, perhaps because she felt refreshed. That was when Mal-Ja entered through the front gate in a hurry. "I got ready early in the morning, but I was only able to arrive now," she said.

"You must have been tending to the needs of your parents-in-law, so how could you expect to leave early?"

"Well, we had a hard time giving your mother a bath just now," said the housekeeper.

"Father, you should have waited until I came. Why do you always do that?"

It seemed like his daughter felt guilty for not coming sooner, and she went into the room and tugged the corners of her mother's blanket to adjust it.

"I've been taking care of your mother all this time. When did you and your sisters have the time? Anyway, what is this absurd idea about you immigrating to the United States?"

"To answer that question and more, Tae-Hyun's father will be here. He'll probably come before lunchtime."

"I don't know. I'm sure you two know how to take care of yourselves. But I'm worried about you living in a strange and foreign country. Did your parents-in-law give you permission?"

"Yes," she said, "though his parents also disapproved at first. When his sister, who lives in America, called and wrote letters to them, they must have changed their minds and decided to see things our way."

When Mr. Kim and Mal-Ja were talking, his wife must have heard their voices and indicated to them that she wanted to sit up. And when Mal-Ja quickly sat her straight up, the grandmother offered her hands out to Mal-Ja to have her nails cut.

Whenever his wife takes a bath, she always has her fingernails and toenails trimmed right afterward. Every time she insisted that only her mother, her daughter, or her husband could cut them for her, not even a middle-aged woman in the neighborhood who offered many times.

When Mal-Ja finished cutting her fingernails onto the newspaper that was spread out, Grandmother Kim must have felt good, for she stuck out one of her feet in front of her. As if treating a child, Mal-Ja started cutting her mother's toenails. But when Grandmother Kim wanted to stick out her left foot, she couldn't make even one movement. As she watched her log-like leg with no sensation, tears fell drop by drop. Tears flowed also from Mal-Ja's eyes, and she turned her face away. At that moment, they heard the noise of someone coming in. It was Won-Ku Lee, Mal-Ja's husband.

"I wanted to come as quickly as possible, but something came up at the press. Father, sir, I apologize."

Won-Ku was brimming over in height and large in physique; he had to bend almost his entire body to get through the low door. When he entered the room and straightened up, the room all of a sudden seemed to have shrunken in size. He bowed in respect to his father-in-law.

"Oh, that's unnecessary," Mr. Kim said. "Your wife also came a few minutes ago."

"What? I'd told you to get ready early. Father, this is entirely my fault. Is my mother-in-law feeling better?"

"As a matter of fact, she just cried when she saw her daughter. This is all an indication that her consciousness is returning, isn't it?" Mr. Kim made an effort to smile.

"Uh, you must have heard from Tae-Hyun's mother, but before the end of this year we are planning to move to the United States. I'm just sorry for everything, Father."

"What are you sorry about? This is the way people lead their lives. Anyway, wherever you go, just do your best. Isn't that enough? Some people even intentionally seek for suffering just to experience it. I'm just worried about the severe hardship you will have to endure with your wife and children in a foreign country."

When Mal-Ja said she wanted to marry Won-Ku Lee, Mr. Kim of course opposed, same as the previous three times when his other daughters married. Won-Ku's family did not have much to begin with, so he finished college by delivering newspapers and tutoring students. Mr. Kim also disapproved because Won-Ku was a newspaper journalist earning a salary man's wages, and he had a father who had back problems and a mother who was constantly ill.

Mr. Kim, who loved his youngest child, Mal-Ja, the one with the tender heart and soft disposition, had been considering having her and her family live at home with him and his wife. But now they were thinking about emigrating, and his heart was in a state of unspeakable grief.

"Father, when I was reading the newspaper a while ago, I saw a lot of elderly people with disabilities like our mother-in-law living in the States. Anyway, they have what is called a wheelchair, an automated chair. Amazingly, by the push of a button, a person can go anywhere he wants to. When we go to the United States, we will find out about it, first thing," said Won-Ku.

"You don't need to do that, but I appreciate you mentioning it."

Mal-Ja's husband left when evening arrived, and the housekeeper left after having dinner prepared.

Today of all days, Grandmother Kim's appetite seemed to have improved because she was able to at least scoop up spoonful of rice with one hand. Even a month ago, when Mr. Kim placed rice and bits of side dishes on her spoon, she was barely able to bring it to her mouth. Now, she was able to scoop the rice, and he only had to place bits of the side dishes on top. It was all thanks to the acupuncture she had been receiving.

When his wife finished dinner, she watched television for about thirty minutes and indicated that she wanted to lie down. Today there were no sports games on, so it seemed like she wasn't enjoying it. Out of all the sports competitions, she liked soccer the most. When the men kicked the soccer ball vigorously, his wife, who was mistaking their kicking for hers, moved her bottom in an itching fashion, expressing great pleasure. When he was about to lay her down on the bed, there was a phone call from Tok-Hee, his second-oldest daughter.

"Father, I heard that Mal-Ja stopped by today."

"Yes, she came with Mr. Lee. You said you weren't feeling well. Are you okay?"

"It's just fatigue from working overtime. Anyway, uh, Father? It's nothing really, but a middle-aged woman from our neighborhood said she wanted to introduce someone who can help take care of Mother."

"That's very good news."

"But her age is a problem."

"Age doesn't matter. It's all right as long as she is healthy and she can stay for a long time."

"She's seventy-two years old. But she's sharp, conscientious, and meticulous, and she has no family. She would live in the house as if it were her own."

"Wait a minute, at that age—how can you even consider that as a possibility?" Mr. Kim stopped himself from saying more.

"I realize that. In any case, I'll find out more about it and tell you in person."

After he received that phone call from Tok-Hee, Mr. Kim felt anger swelling up inside. He knew that they were talking about finding someone who could take care of a paralyzed person, but he wondered, *What can a seventy-year-old person do?* He became disappointed and went so far as to entertain insolent thoughts.

His friends and neighbors often talked about Mr. Kim and expressed their empathy. The women from the Chungpadong marketplace were saying things like, "It must seem bleak to have a wife who's in that condition, at his age!" "I know what you mean. It's too bad for the husband. It should be the wife who needs to be more healthy and live longer than the husband." "Why are you sympathizing? Are you by any chance harboring ill will?" They continued to whisper.

It was only two months since his wife collapsed. A friend and occasional drinking partner whom he met at a senior citizen association told Mr. Kim that he'd be willing to volunteer as a matchmaker and formally introduce him to an eligible woman. She was thirty-seven years old, an old miss who wouldn't expect anything other than to have a married life with somebody in their declining years and depend on each other.

People usually still see men in their sixties as quite robust, and this was the case for the sixty-five-year-old Mr. Kim, who looked ten years younger than his actual age. But this didn't change the fact that his wife was still alive, and there were rows after rows of his daughters' children and their children's children. He took what his friend told him only as something said in passing. However, in one corner of his heart, something could not be pinpointed, but a sticky emptiness lay motionless within.

Tok-Hee, who did not understand what was in Mr.

Kim's heart, ran into the house to discuss the matter of the seventy-year-old grandmother.

"Did you take some time to think about it?"

"I know it's hard to find someone, but how could I leave your mother in the hands of a seventy-year-old grandmother? Even though it's hard now, it's better to go on living like this."

"Father, that's fine, but how long can you go on like this, as you said? When winter comes, how will you manage? Your daughters are also in the same position. We promised to take turns to look after Mother, but look at Mal-Ja's older sister, for instance. She said she would come from Suyuri at two in the morning, but just how early can she actually get here?" Tok-Hee already spoke in a half-threatening manner.

The seventy-year-old grandmother was a widow who barely made a living doing needlework with her only daughter. Eventually her daughter came of age, and it was time for her to get married, which meant the grandmother would lose her daughter. But her daughter at least lived close by, so the grandmother was able to derive a sense of purpose for living. However, when the daughter's husband signed a three-year contract working for his company on the construction site of a road at Kwam-to, the grandmother was naturally separated from her daughter. The daughter said she would be back in three years, but there was no news from her ever since. Then the grandmother's eyesight became dimmer and dimmer, and soon she was unable to do any needlework.

"Father, I think that's why, for mother's sake, the

seventy-year-old grandmother would actually be the better choice. This grandmother isn't planning on going anywhere, so things will turn out for the better."

Tok-Hee was treating them like senior citizens because in reality they were old, but Mr. Kim did not have anything to say.

Mr. Kim was thinking that there was not much he could do about it and didn't respond. There's an old saying that even a wicked wife who's despised is better than ten filial sons, and that was exactly the case. This does not mean his wife was a wicked woman, nor was she a content mother. There was not one day when she was at peace with herself because she felt guilty and responsible for not being able to give birth to a son. They say that a woman's jealousy is like white frost that falls in May and June, and his wife's jealousy did not fade as she aged.

That was the case even before his wife collapsed. Since Ms. Park worked at a cabaret, her job required her to go out in the evenings and return the next day at daybreak. It was only natural for Mr. Kim, who did not sleep at dawn or during the morning hours, to open the door for her. Since Ms. Park felt bad, she bought him cigarettes and liquor. Even though Grandmother Kim understood her sentiments almost perfectly, some of the women with big mouths spread rumors that led to wild imagination in the minds of strangers.

Grandmother Kim became suspicious of almost everything, and Ms. Park couldn't stand her bullet stares. Ms. Park was about to move to a room in a different house, but that was when the accident happened.

Within a couple of days Mr. Kim, who mulled over the issue of hiring a grandmother, finally gave his daughters his approval. The seventy-something-year-old grandmother carried one bundle and followed Tok-Hee into his house, and she did not look as repulsive and old as he had imagined. She looked far younger than her actual age.

As soon as she moved into the house, the atmosphere changed in one day. She washed the bundled-up blankets, organized the insides of the closets, thoroughly wiped off the accumulated dust from every corner of the kitchen, and in short the house looked brighter. Mr. Kim was able to meet with his friend and drink liquor with a relaxed mind. But once his body relaxed, his heart felt lonelier in any circumstance. Conversely, when his body and mind were busy, there was no room or time to think about how lonely and distressed he was.

As autumn's bright and fair weather passed and winter stood at the threshold, Mr. Kim's heart became troubled. Winter always provided unfavorable conditions for the elderly; when the cold wind blew, limbs that used to be healthy become painful in the joints. He felt the nothingness of human existence. There was no particular place to go, but staying at home became suffocating, so Mr. Kim immediately left the house for the neighborhood tavern.

In Seoul he had a few friends, but he could not visit them that easily because they lived with their sons' or daughters' families. Nevertheless, there was one friend who lived only with his wife, but he lived in the high-rise apartments. Going up and down the staircases and the small space of his friend's apartment made Mr. Kim feel suffocated, as if someone blocked his breathing.

Inside the tavern, business was slow—perhaps because it was still morning. Mr. Kim was purposely looking for a secluded place to sit, but Madame Song was delighted to see him and came over.

"My goodness! What's the occasion, Mr. Kim? You've come all the way here! Has your wife's health improved?"

"I wish it were a disease that could be easily cured. Anyway, how are you, Madame Song?"

"I wish there was something financially stable about selling liquor. Anyway, Mr. Kim, you must be having a hard time, but what can be done? There's nothing anyone can do about what happened, but at the same time, how can you live with such loneliness?"

He wasn't sure whether Madame Song was genuinely concerned or not, but her face became pale as she spoke. For a woman way over thirty, Madame Song was not strikingly beautiful but had a well-developed figure. Her eyes were inviting, and she was overall an attractive woman.

Today of all days, Mr. Kim appreciated and was particularly in need of Madame Song's words. If it had been any other time, he would have taken her words lightly, absentmindedly made jokes, and overlooked it, but today that was not the case. In fact, he became jealous when she looked at other customers. Madame Song was slowly cracking open Mr. Kim's heart as she selectively chose only sweet words to flow out of her mouth.

"In any case, even though Mrs. Kim is lying down all the time, she must be very happy. If I met a husband like you, I would be going around giving him a piggyback ride."

"You don't need to go that far. I'm only doing the right thing. Anyway, did Mr. Park stop by here, by any chance?"

"My God! You didn't hear about the news? He suffered from high blood pressure and passed away about a month ago."

When Mr. Kim heard about Mr. Park's death, he felt his heart writhing in pain. Mr. Park was someone he'd gotten to know when he bought the house in Chungpadong, someone he'd called upon quite often. But after Grandmother Kim collapsed, it became naturally hard for him to see his friend, and he could not go anywhere because he was unable to find anyone to work around the house. Therefore, during all this time, Mr. Kim did not know what had happened.

Mr. Park, who was close to seventy, was a rich man. He was the owner of a couple of houses in one neighborhood in the town of Namyong. According to his stories, ever since his wife died five years ago, he'd been living in one son's house after another, but his heart was not at peace. Even though it would have been difficult to live alone, he told them that was what he'd wanted. In any case, it seemed like the struggles waged within his heart were too much for him to bear.

"And so what I'm saying is all that money was useless. He was playing the role of a stingy father toward his sons, and what kind of son would like that?" said Madame Song.

"That's probably because he wanted what was best for his sons. Anyway, it's now the sons' responsibilities."

"If he was kindhearted toward his sons from the beginning, he would have been treated well."

"So what you're saying is things turned out this way because he moved out and lived alone?"

"Of course not. He couldn't even move out. He went to live with one son after another, and finally his last day came. So it seems useless to have many sons. It's better to have one son, and even better to have daughters. When I see his sons losing love for humanity and not taking responsibility, I fully realize the truth behind the saying that being childless is good fortune. I think when a man is young he should be good to his wife, even with the smallest things, so that when they get old, he will not become an unpredictable fool."

Madame Song spoke excitedly, as if it were her own problem. But Mr. Kim heard her words as if she had sat him down and spoke directly to him, and they burned his heart. His wife said that she wanted to live in a quiet place, but he did not spend the property money a little at a time and thought he'd collect one more penny. But eventually, everything collapsed, and he felt responsible for the entire mess.

"If human life is preordained by the heavens, then can it turn into a life engineered by man's will?" asked Mr. Kim. "I was wondering because it's extremely frustrating to see a person who's been so healthy all his life and all of a sudden become so sick."

"Mr. Kim, don't be heartbroken by your wife's tragic

misfortune. Instead you should enjoy everything around you and eat whatever your heart desires. And you never know. Mrs. Kim might all of a sudden stand up again—"

"Well, that's what should be happening. But looking at things now—in any case, since you are worrying about me like this, Madame Song, my heart feels like it has all of a sudden become liberated, and it feels good."

"Oh, really? Since we've brought up the subject, if there is a place you'd like to go for fun, will you please take me with you? These days I haven't been taking it easy, myself."

By noon, customers came in by ones and twos, and it began to get very busy for Madame Song. Thinking it useless for him to just sit there, Mr. Kim stood up and left.

Outside, it was already broad daylight, and the hot rays of the sun spilled on top of his head, making him feel slightly dizzy. *Where should I go?* he wondered. but his feet were taking him toward his home in no time.

Mr. Kim's work each day wasn't much, but time passed by so fast, as if someone was eating it up. Before long, the harshness of winter was settling in and taking over the morning and night. The cold wind blew on the surface of his clothes, but even the insides of his bones felt the chill. The conversations of the women living in the neighborhood became extensive. They were talking about how so-and-so already prepared their pickled vegetables for the winter, how the price of condiments and spices rose tremendously since last year, how the price of cabbage became so ridiculously expensive that they'll probably eat "gold kimchi," and so on.

That did not mean that the Kim's family wasn't going to eat kimchi and wasn't preparing the necessary ingredients. When Mr. Kim was thinking that he had to do it for his wife's sake, Tok-Hee called.

"Father, I know that our family is small, but don't you think we should prepare about thirty heads of cabbage?"

"Well, I won't be eating much, but shouldn't we make it anyway since your mother is here?"

"So I was thinking that this coming Sunday, we could prepare kimchi."

"Why? All of you should make it at home first. It's okay if we prepare it at my place later."

"Well, I think we should have it done at your place first so we would feel better. Please keep this in mind."

"Then, we'll do it that way. This coming Saturday, I'll have the cabbages brought here so all of you can just come on Sunday without having to prepare much. It's already not easy for all of you to come out here."

"Will that be okay with you?"

"Yeah, of course it is. It doesn't matter who buys the cabbages."

"Then, can you please do that? I'll buy the spices early Sunday morning. And can you please turn me over to Mother?"

When her mother got on the phone, Tok-Hee told her about what was going on.

Whether it is a lot or a little amount of work, people are alike in that they have a tendency not to skip any step of a routine process unless they want to disrupt their lives. As soon as Mr. Kim got off the phone with Tok-Hee, he went to the Chungpadong market to find out about the price and quality of cabbages. If the leaves of the cabbages were thin, then they didn't look fresh and did not have much inside or enough leaves. If the size of the cabbage was just right, then the leaves were tough and didn't look that tasty. In the end, he wasn't sure which one to choose, so he asked the man to bring the cabbages to his house, the one who pulled a cart around the neighborhood to sell food. At the break of dawn on Sunday, he went to the Chungpadong market to buy spices. He knew that his daughters would take care of everything once they arrived, but he had the desire to help with even the smallest task. Again he was at a loss, unsure of what to buy. About a year ago, he never really paid attention to his wife when she was preparing to pickle cabbages, since he was just disinterested. But now his inner realization that he had to take care of every little detail of his and her life, such as what to eat and what to wear, abruptly made sorrow well up inside of him.

In the marketplace at dawn, as soon as the goods were brought in, the line would immediately become long. At that time, he saw a woman, a little over thirty years old, was doing food shopping, so he went up to ask her for help.

"My God! Mr. Kim, are you actually food shopping? Where is your wife? Oh, I mean, don't you have daughters-in-law?"

"My daughters said that they were coming over. Instead of staying home idly, I thought I'd come out here to find out about the cost of thirty heads of cabbage and spices, but I'm having a hard time."

"Don't worry about that. I need about thirty heads of cabbage too. Just follow me when I buy things, and you'll be fine. I assume that your wife must have passed away already? Maybe you also don't have sons."

Even though this woman was food shopping, she must have been curious about Mr. Kim because she kept asking questions. The women who were selling food and goods in baskets stared at him behind their sale items, looking him up and down, regardless how he felt about their stares. These women were hard manual laborers who were working with everything they had to make a living. Fascinated by Mr. Kim, a man shopping for food, they continued staring at him. Mr. Kim, who'd gone to the market in a frenzy so early in the morning, in the end gave up shopping and decided to go home to prepare beef spare rib soup for his daughters instead.

Tok-Hee and Mal-Ja came early in the morning, and so did Su-Hee. When it was noon, Kum-Ja came stumbling in.

"Being a teacher doesn't give you the excuse to be late." Tok-Hee, who was washing the cabbage, scolded Kum-Ja with a disapproving look on her face.

"Oh, sis, do you think I'm comfortable about this?"

"Now that we're on the topic, let me ask you. How many times have you come to see Mother?"

"Why are you guys doing this again? You know how I feel about all this." Su-Hee, who was sweeping with a broom, thought that this couldn't go on and interrupted the conversation.

"Then what am I? I also have work to do around my

house that's a mountain high. As a matter of fact, we all know that our older sister can't help it because she lives far away. Kum-Ja can't help it because of school. Mal-Ja will be emigrating in the future, and we don't know what her exact plans are, so why are we even bothering to talk about this when we know each other's circumstances?" Tok-Hee, who had these words bottled up inside her heart for some time, now brought it out with no reins holding her back.

A little while before, Mr. Kim felt a sense of relieved happiness growing within for having all of his daughters together, but soon he regretted what his burdensome existence was doing to them.

Su-Hee had washed the radish through a sieve and was putting salted eggs, ground red pepper, scallion, and garlic on top of it and mixing it when an old hometown friend of Mr. Kim, Mr. To-Kye, came to the house.

"Wait a minute! What's the occasion for all of you? Is that you, Mal-Ja? Tok-Hee's here too. Everyone's here. You must have all come to prepare kimchi. Of course, that's right—you should. Mal-Ja, you now show signs of a mother handling couple of kids. Yes, how time flies. It's scary, really scary."

When Grandfather To-Kye saw his friend's daughters, it must have brought back old memories, for it shook his concept of an uncertain life and soaked him in sentimental recollections of his past. It was no surprise because when the fourth daughter was born, it was Mr. To-Kye Chang himself who had given her the name Mal-Ja, with hopes that she would stop taking care of additional younger sisters.

"What's the occasion? Coming all the way to my house? Hurry up and go inside," said Mr. Kim.

"Excuse me, Pyong-Ju Kim. I might have been busy with my nose running all over the place, but how about you? Why haven't you even called once?"

When Grandfather To-Kye went into the room, Tok-Hee gave him a dirty look. She had her reasons for doing that. It took Grandfather To-Kye a whole month just to pay a visit to see their mother since she was out of the hospital.

"Now, about your father. How could he go on living like this? You should be able to read your father's mind. This is making a blunt remark, but if we don't take personal care of each other, then aren't we like dead bodies?"

"Sir, just what exactly are you trying to say?" The light in Tok-Hee's eyes burned and crackled.

"No, it's nothing. I was just saying that's the way things are."

"Sir, your words sound like they have seeds of loaded meaning. It hasn't been that long since Mother collapsed, so how can you be saying such things?"

It must have been uncomfortable even for quiet Su-Hee, the oldest daughter, to listen to this, so she tried to help ease the tension. She stopped what she was doing and prepared the beef rib soup with leafy greens and brought out a small portable table. Grandmother Kim also must have been excited on a day like this because she didn't think about lying down to rest.

"Hey, I haven't been saying anything all this time, but no one would have guessed that I was boiling up inside."

"You? Why? You have a fresh, young wife. And you're under the care of your strong son. What more are you looking for?"

"Of course, compared to you, I may sound like someone who should be brimming over with many blessings. But do you think just because someone lives with his son, he ought to be happy? It all depends on what kind of son he has."

"Why? What's wrong with your son, Chun-Tae?"

"He said he was running a so-called business, but he lost all of his property. Now, that bastard's business is a supermarket, and wouldn't you know it? It's a business that sucks the flesh off of you. My wife is on my back, trying to hassle me to find an apartment. Chun-Tae thinks it was a big deal for him to support his younger sister through school, but you already know what kind of money he used to start his business, right? Mine! And now he's making a big commotion, bragging about his heroic deeds, and I am totally dumbfounded from disbelief. The townspeople, who had no clue as to how we felt, were pointing their fingers and passing judgment on us, saying that I was involved with a young woman and causing my old wife to shrivel up with more wrinkles. So would you call this living? I don't think so. It's hell."

"Of course that's something that deserves finger-pointing. If your wife was even three or four years older than Chun-Tae, then they wouldn't be saying such things."

"Now you're on my case too? It's all because of fate."

"How could you call it fate? Isn't it because you like young women?"

"Hah! I can't believe these people," he shook his head. "Can you really make someone suffer by pushing all the wrong buttons?"

"I was just making a comment. Anyway, is your business going well?"

"That so-called supermarket is a shining wild apricot that isn't as good as it looks. Since a delivery on any given day takes such a long time, it's better to have a small store about the size of a hole in the wall. And there is such a thing as a delivery, which only makes crumb-like change. Of course the body and mind take a great toll in the process."

"Well, that just depends on the business. If it does well, then Chun-Tae will automatically know the right time and occasion to buy a house for you. You have to be patient until that time. What can you do? You must know his intentions better than anyone else."

"Of course, why shouldn't I know how he feels? These days it's pathetic to watch Mi-Hae's mother, my new wife. As I was saying, these days I am actually envious of you."

"Me? How can you say such a thing? It's better to curse me."

"I'm being honest. It would have been better to have Chun-Tae's mother sick with a disability than to have her still be alive. Then there wouldn't be this kind of humiliation and suffering." In the end, Grandfather To-Kye showed trickles of tears, some of which he swallowed.

"Hey. If a person does not experience it for himself, then he can't possibly understand my position," Mr. Kim informed Grandfather To-Kye. "It's because I haven't said anything, but how could anyone call this living? This is barely living. Anyway, now that Mal-Ja has decided to immigrate to America—"

"Wait, why is Mal-Ja all of a sudden saying that she's going? It would make sense if someone she knows already lives there."

"Her older sister-in-law who is there keeps telling her to come. In any case, she is leaving pretty soon."

"Now that I think about it, you'll have a chance to go to America because of her, so what are you complaining about?"

"Hold on. How can you say such things at a time like this?"

"What is it with you? Don't you know that these days parents who have daughters are the most content and the most fortunate? You know the saying, that it's the parents and not the parents-in-law who get to go to America. Anyway, don't be distressed because you only have daughters. At least daughters are the only ones who truly understand their parents. How is your son-in-law? Isn't he good to your daughter?"

Grandmother Kim, who was next to him, was diligently watching TV, unaware of what was going on, but all of a sudden her facial expression indicated that she was about to cry. At that moment, Mr. Kim lifted the small table of liquor and went into the next room. It was because his wife was about to go to the bathroom soon.

Grandfather To-Kye must have read his mind and figured that staying long wasn't a good idea, so he soon got up and left.

When Grandfather To-Kye left, they almost finished

preparing the kimchi, and the clamor of washing dishes made the house sound alive. It was getting dark, and when evening came, everyone went home in ones and twos. Then only a quiet stillness filled the room.

About four days later, Mr. Kim left the house with a free and easy spirit. It was because for four whole days, something that Grandfather To-Kye said was roaming around in his mind.

"I think Madame Song is, without a doubt, very interested in you. If that wasn't the case, then why would she worry about you like that?"

On this particular day, the sky looked as if snow was about to fall, expressing its lingering state. On such a day, he couldn't stand to stay home any longer, with his arms and legs almost frozen.

When he walked into the tavern, all of a sudden it felt rather cold, and Madame Song was nowhere in sight. So he discreetly inquired her whereabouts.

"Sister Madame Song probably won't be in for a few days."

"Why? Is she not feeling well?"

"No, it's not that. Her husband, who went to Vietnam, came back. I heard they might transfer this tavern on to another owner, but I'm not sure."

Mr. Kim put his cup down and politely volunteered some extra information.

Ever since he stepped into the tavern, it felt cold. A strange emotion settled within. Something like this was bound to happen. Then Mr. Kim felt ashamed and betrayed and didn't have one clue about what to do next.

During all this time, even though thoughts of Madame Song were all in his mind, he still couldn't reconcile the conflicts of his heart. Since he felt as if someone was peeping at his heart, he drank his coffee and left the tavern immediately. When he came out, there was actually no place for him to go. He absentmindedly walked around the streets of the town of Namyong. The streets were so busy with crowds of people that they pushed Mr. Kim, who was walking feebly. They even broke out in a fit of annoyed rage at him.

"This is life, with nothing particularly special about it," he mumbled to himself, and then suddenly he stared at a tree in the street. The tree was able to endure even harsh winters. When spring came, it turned shiny green and dewy, something that, out of the blue, made him feel envious. He thought to himself, *Wouldn't it be great if youth could come once again to men?* He was also thinking, as if there were still some lingering attachments, *When I leave this world, I should depart with no emotional attachments or longings. Of course that's what going to happen.* He was thinking this as if he was actually mentally practicing to leave, tenaciously and ruthlessly rounding up all the fleeing elements of his heart.

Two months later, it was February and the dead of winter. Mal-Ja's family finished all the preparations for their emigration, and soon it was time for them to leave. As Mal-Ja was organizing this and that in her house, a thought must have occurred to her, because she brought a dresser to Mr. Kim's house, something her mother bought for her when she married and left the family to join her in-laws.

Mal-Ja's intention was to have Grandmother Kim admire the dresser as if it was her daughter, but Grandmother Kim, not knowing what was going on, simply seemed to like having it there. Two days before Mal-Ja's family had to leave for the United States, Su-Hee took matters into her own hands and prepared a nice dinner. Soon it seemed as if the room was like the inside of an earthenware steamer full of bean sprouts, crowded and swarming with people and noise. Grandmother Kim, not knowing the reason for the occasion, liked the fact that everyone had gathered, and she beamed. However, after finding out that it was a farewell party, she started weeping loudly. It was not the sound of a human cry—more like the guttural cry of a bull being dragged to a slaughterhouse.

Soon the room became a sea of tears. Mr. Kim also couldn't prevent himself from crying, so he went outside into the yard. A cold wind blew and grazed his face, and his senses were abruptly awakened. Nevertheless, realizing that there wasn't even one place on this land where he could comfortably cry as he wanted, he felt cornered into a suffocating explosion of wailing and agonizing groans. He thought that maybe until he died he would not have an opportunity to cry as freely as he wanted.

The honorable white moon in the mud-painted sky, which seemed to ponder upon Mr. Kim's heart, stood aloof.

Two days later, Mr. Kim went to Kimpo Airport to send off Mal-Ja and her family. There were times when mostly people left to go abroad as coal miners in West Germany, or immigrants to Brazil, and so on. There were also many people going abroad because of the Vietnam War, but when the year 1975 came around, people were forming lines to immigrate to the United States.

Mal-Ja and her husband checked their luggage, and as they drew closer to Mr. Kim, they hesitated to speak.

Not being able to tolerate the silence, Mal-Ja said, "Father, I remember what you used to tell me a long time ago. No matter where a person is in this world, he must keep his promises. So I am leaving, knowing that I can trust you."

Mal-Ja mentioned this because she was worried that her father might leave her mother and by chance remarry.

Then an announcement from the loudspeaker echoed in all directions, saying that the plane was about to take off. Mr. Kim thought, *Now this is the moment of truth, the actual time of departure,* and his heart made a splash and then subsided. Mal-Ja went to the departure gate at last, and her frowning face, which was on the brink of tears, became a hazy image on the lenses of his glasses that enlarged and then soon evaporated. For a moment, Mr. Kim became stupefied and felt dizzy. But thinking that he had to say something, he gathered and shaped his lips to speak.

"Hey, how could I pretend as if I don't care about your mother, who has been washing my smelly underwear and stinky socks for forty years? How can you say that you know what's in my heart?" However, they were words that wandered around and around his mind and could not be formulated into spoken words.

The airplane let out an incredibly loud combustion noise and ripped into the sky, soon disappearing into the clouds. In the gray sky, the white gas trailed a long tail that soon vanished without a trace. *I will also depart like that. Of course I will, without a doubt.*

Mr. Kim, feeling as though he was also taking off into the sky, tightly closed both of his eyes for a long time.

greenartschool@yahoo.com

Printed in the United States
By Bookmasters

NEW YORK LITERATURE

NEW YORK LITERATURE

A Collection of Poems, Essays, and Stories

Korean American Writers Asso.of E. USA

Copyright © 2015 Korean American Writers Association of Eastern USA.

All rights reserved. No part of this book may be used or reproduced by any means, graphic, electronic, or mechanical, including photocopying, recording, taping or by any information storage retrieval system without the written permission of the author except in the case of brief quotations embodied in critical articles and reviews.

This is a work of fiction. All of the characters, names, incidents, organizations, and dialogue in this novel are either the products of the author's imagination or are used fictitiously.

Archway Publishing books may be ordered through booksellers or by contacting:

Archway Publishing
1663 Liberty Drive
Bloomington, IN 47403
www.archwaypublishing.com
1 (888) 242-5904

Because of the dynamic nature of the Internet, any web addresses or links contained in this book may have changed since publication and may no longer be valid. The views expressed in this work are solely those of the author and do not necessarily reflect the views of the publisher, and the publisher hereby disclaims any responsibility for them.

Any people depicted in stock imagery provided by Thinkstock are models, and such images are being used for illustrative purposes only. Certain stock imagery © Thinkstock.

ISBN: 978-1-4808-2580-2 (sc)
ISBN: 978-1-4808-2581-9 (e)

Library of Congress Control Number: 2015920935

Print information available on the last page.

Archway Publishing rev. date: 12/23/2015